"Stunning . . . *The Things They Carried* is about the power of the imagination . . . I've read all five of O'Brien's books with admiration that sometimes verges on awe. Nobody else can make me feel . . . what I imagine to have been the reality of that war."            — *USA Today*

"Powerful . . . Composed in the same lean, vigorous style as his earlier books, *The Things They Carried* adds up to a captivating account of the experiences of an infantry company in Vietnam . . . Evocative and haunting, the raw force of confession."            — *Wall Street Journal*

"O'Brien has written a book so searing and immediate you can almost hear the choppers in the background. Drenched in irony and purple-haze napalm, the Vietnam narrative has almost been forced to produce a new kind of war literature. *The Things They Carried* is an extraordinary contribution to that class of fiction . . . It leaves third-degree burns. Between its rhythmic brilliance and its exquisite rendering of memory . . . this is prose headed for the nerve center of what was Vietnam."   — *Boston Globe*

"The best of these stories—and none is written with less than the sharp edge of honed vision—are memory as prophecy. They tell us not where we were but where we are, and perhaps where we will be . . . It is an ultimate, indelible image of war in our time, and in time to come."
            — *Los Angeles Times*

"O'Brien adds his second title to the short list of essential fiction about Vietnam . . . By moving beyond the horror of the fighting to examine with sensitivity and insight the nature of courage and fear, by questioning the role that imagination plays in helping to form our memories and our own versions of truth, he places *The Things They Carried* high up on the list of best fiction about any war . . . A stunning performance. The overall effect of these original tales is devastating." —*New York Times Book Review*

"The integrity of a novel and the immediacy of an autobiography . . . giving us a deep sense of the fluidity of truth and the dance of memory." —*The New Yorker*

"When *Going After Cacciato* appeared out of nowhere to win the 1979 National Book Award, it seemed to many, myself included, that no finer fiction had, as of then, been written in the closing half of the 20th century—or was likely to be in the remaining years to come. *The Things They Carried* disposes of that prediction . . . O'Brien is the best American writer of his generation."
—*San Francisco Examiner*

"*The Things They Carried* is as good as any piece of literature can get . . . It is the perfect approach to this sort of material, and O'Brien does it with vast skill and grace . . . It is controlled and wild, deep and tough, perceptive and shrewd. I salute the man who wrote it."
—*Chicago Sun-Times*

"This is writing so powerful that it steals your breath . . . It perfectly captures the moral confusion that is the legacy of the Vietnam War . . . *The Things They Carried* is about more than war, of course. It is about the human heart and emotional baggage and loyalty and love. It is about the difference between 'truth' and 'reality.' It is about death—and life. It is successful on every level."
—*Milwaukee Journal*

"I've got to make you read this book . . . A certain panic arises in me. In trying to review a book as precious as *The Things They Carried* by Tim O'Brien, there is the nightmare fear of saying the wrong thing—of not getting the book's wonder across to you fairly—and of sounding merely zealous, fanatical, and hence to be dismissed. If I can't get you to go out and buy this book, then I've failed you . . . In a world filled too often with numbness, or shifting values, these stories shine in a strange and opposite direction, moving against the flow, illuminating life's wonder, life's tenuousness, life's importance."

—*Dallas Morning News*

"Consummate artistry . . . A strongly unified book, a series of glimpses, through different facets, of a single, mysterious, deadly stone . . . O'Brien blends diverse incidents, voices, and genres, indelibly rendering the nightmarish impact of the Vietnam experience."

—*Philadelphia Inquirer*

"Simply marvelous . . . A striking sequence of stories that twist and turn and bounce off each other . . . Wars seldom produce good short stories, but two or three of these seem as good as any short stories written about any war . . . Immensely affecting."

—*Newsweek*

"O'Brien has brought us another remarkable piece of work . . . The stories have a specificity of observed physical detail that makes them seem a model of the realist's art."

—*Miami Herald*

"Even more than *Cacciato*, *The Things They Carried* is virtually impossible to summarize in conventional terms. If anything, it is a better book . . . The novel is held together by two things: the haunting clarity of O'Brien's prose and the intensity of his focus . . . O'Brien's stories are like nobody else's. His blend of poetic realism and comic fantasy remains unique . . . His Vietnam stories are really about the yearning for peace—aimed at human understanding rather than some 'definitive' understanding of the war . . . O'Brien can bring it all back. He can feel the terror and the sorrow and the crazy, jagged laughter. He can bring the dead back to life. And bring back the dreaming, too."

—*Entertainment Weekly*

"O'Brien has unmistakably forged one of the most persuasive works of any kind to arise out of any war."

—*Hartford Courant*

"O'Brien succeeds as well as any writer in conveying the free-fall sensation of fear and the surrealism of combat."

—*Time*

"It's a marvelous and chilling book, and something totally new in fiction. A dramatic redefinition of fiction itself, maybe. It will probably be a bestseller and a movie, and deserves to be. It will be nominated for prizes, but I wonder if any prize will do it justice. Maybe a silver star for telling the truth that never happened, passionately, gracefully."

—*Charlotte Observer*

"*The Things They Carried* carries not only the soldiers' intangible burdens—grief, terror, love, longing—but also the weight of memory, the terrible gravity of guilt. It carries them, though, with a lovely, stirring grace, because it is as much about the redemptive power of stories as it is about Vietnam."

—*Orlando Sentinel*

"A master stroke of form and imagery . . . O'Brien tells us these stories because he must. He tells them as they have never been told before . . . If *Cacciato* was the book about Vietnam, then this is the book about surviving it."
— *Richmond Times-Dispatch*

"One hell of a book . . . You'll rarely read anything as real as this."
— *St. Louis Post-Dispatch*

"Throughout, it is incredibly ordinary, human stuff— that's why this book is extra-ordinary . . . Each story resonates with its predecessors, yet stands alone."
— *Houston Chronicle*

"Astonishing . . . Richly wrought and filled with war's paradoxes, *The Things They Carried* will reward a second, or even a third, reading . . . His ambitious, modernistic fable, *Going After Cacciato*, raised the American war novel to new artistic realms. *The Things They Carried* is also astonishing—in a whole new way."
— *Boston Sunday Herald*

"Eloquent . . . O'Brien expertly fires off tracer rounds, illuminating the art of war in all its horrible and fascinating complexity, detailing the mad and the mundane . . . *The Things They Carried* joins the work of Crane and Hemingway and Mailer as great war literature."
— *Tampa Tribune & Times*

"*The Things They Carried* is distinguished by virtue of the novelty and complexity of its presentation. O'Brien is a superb prose stylist, perhaps the best among Vietnam War novelists . . . The imaginative retelling of the war is just as real as the war itself, maybe more so, and experiencing these narratives can be powerfully cathartic for writer and reader alike."

—*Atlanta Journal & Constitution*

"The search for the great American novel will never end, but it gets a step closer to realization with *The Things They Carried*."

—*Detroit Free Press*

"The writing is as clear as one of his northern Minnesota lakes . . . This is one of those books you should read. It is also one of those books you'll be glad you did . . . This book—and these lives—will live for a long time."

—*Milwaukee Sentinel*

"There have been movies. And plays. And books. But there has been nothing like Tim O'Brien's *The Things They Carried* . . . All of us, by holding O'Brien's stories in our hands, can approach Vietnam and truth."

—*San Diego Union*

"His characters and his situations are unique and ring true to the point of tears. His prose is simply magnificent . . . Unforgettable."

—*Minneapolis Star Tribune*

"A powerful yet lyrical work of fiction."

—*The Associated Press*

"O'Brien's new master work . . . Go out and get this book and read it. Read it slowly, and let O'Brien's masterful storytelling and his eloquent philosophizing about the nature of war wash over you . . . *The Things They Carried* is a major work of literary imagination."

—*The Veteran*

## Books by Tim O'Brien

# The Things
# They Carried

A WORK OF FICTION BY

## Tim O'Brien

 Mariner Books · Houghton Mifflin Harcourt
BOSTON  NEW YORK

First Mariner Books edition 2009

For information about permission to reproduce selections from this book,
write to Permissions, Houghton Mifflin Harcourt Publishing Company,
215 Park Avenue South, New York, New York 10003.

www.hmhbooks.com

First published in 1990 by Houghton Mifflin

Library of Congress Cataloging-in-Publication Data is available.

ISBN 978-0-618-70641-9

Printed in the United States of America

DOC 10 9 8 7 6 5 4 3 2

Of these stories, five first appeared in *Esquire*: "The Things They Carried,"
"How to Tell a True War Story," "Sweetheart of the Song Tra Bong," "The
Ghost Soldiers," and "The Lives of the Dead." "Speaking of Courage" was
first published in *The Massachusetts Review*, then later, in a revised version,
in *Granta*. "In the Field" was first published in *Gentleman's Quarterly*. "Style,"
"Spin," and "The Man I Killed" were first published, in different form, in *The
Quarterly*. "The Things They Carried" appeared in *The Best American Short
Stories 1987*. "Speaking of Courage" and "The Ghost Soldiers" appeared in
*Prize Stories: The O. Henry Awards* (1978 and 1982). "On the Rainy River"
first appeared in *Playboy*. The author wishes to thank the editors of those
publications and to express gratitude for support received from the National
Endowment for the Arts.

This book is lovingly dedicated to the men of
Alpha Company, and in particular to Jimmy Cross,
Norman Bowker, Rat Kiley, Mitchell Sanders,
Henry Dobbins, and Kiowa.

## ACKNOWLEDGMENTS

My thanks to Erik Hansen, Rust Hills,
Camille Hykes, Seymour Lawrence, Andy McKillop,
Ivan Nabokov, Les Ramirez, and, above all,
to Ann O'Brien.

# Contents

This book is essentially different from any other that has been published concerning the "late war" or any of its incidents. Those who have had any such experience as the author will see its truthfulness at once, and to all other readers it is commended as a statement of actual things by one who experienced them to the fullest.

—*John Ransom's Andersonville Diary*

# THE THINGS
# THEY CARRIED

# The Things They Carried

First Lieutenant Jimmy Cross carried letters from a girl named Martha, a junior at Mount Sebastian College in New Jersey. They were not love letters, but Lieutenant Cross was hoping, so he kept them folded in plastic at the bottom of his rucksack. In the late afternoon, after a day's march, he would dig his foxhole, wash his hands under a canteen, unwrap the letters, hold them with the tips of his fingers, and spend the last hour of light pretending. He would imagine romantic camping trips into the White Mountains in New Hampshire. He would sometimes taste the envelope flaps, knowing her tongue had been there. More than anything, he wanted Martha to love him as he loved her, but the letters were mostly chatty, elusive on the matter of love. She was a virgin, he was almost sure. She was an English major at Mount Sebastian, and she wrote beautifully about her professors and roommates and midterm exams, about her respect for Chaucer and her great affection for Virginia Woolf. She often quoted lines of poetry; she never mentioned the war, except to say, Jimmy, take care of yourself. The letters weighed 4 ounces. They were signed Love, Martha, but Lieutenant Cross understood that Love was only a way of signing and did not mean what he sometimes pretended it meant. At dusk, he would carefully return the letters to his rucksack. Slowly, a bit distracted, he would get up and move among his men, checking the perimeter, then at full dark he would return to his hole and watch the night and wonder if Martha was a virgin.

The things they carried were largely determined by necessity. Among the necessities or near-necessities were P-38 can openers, pocket knives, heat tabs, wristwatches, dog tags, mosquito repellent, chewing gum, candy, cigarettes, salt tablets, packets of Kool-Aid, lighters, matches, sewing kits, Military Payment Certificates, C rations, and two or three canteens of water. Together, these items weighed between 12 and 18 pounds, depending upon a man's habits or rate of metabolism. Henry Dobbins, who was a big man, carried extra rations; he was especially fond of canned peaches in heavy syrup over pound cake. Dave Jensen, who practiced field hygiene, carried a toothbrush, dental floss, and several hotel-sized bars of soap he'd stolen on R&R in Sydney, Australia. Ted Lavender, who was scared, carried tranquilizers until he was shot in the head outside the village of Than Khe in mid-April. By necessity, and because it was SOP, they all carried steel helmets that weighed 5 pounds including the liner and camouflage cover. They carried the standard fatigue jackets and trousers. Very few carried underwear. On their feet they carried jungle boots—2.1 pounds—and Dave Jensen carried three pairs of socks and a can of Dr. Scholl's foot powder as a precaution against trench foot. Until he was shot, Ted Lavender carried 6 or 7 ounces of premium dope, which for him was a necessity. Mitchell Sanders, the RTO, carried condoms. Norman Bowker carried a diary. Rat Kiley carried comic books. Kiowa, a devout Baptist, carried an illustrated New Testament that had been presented to him by his father, who taught Sunday school in Oklahoma City, Oklahoma. As a hedge against bad times, however, Kiowa also carried his grandmother's distrust of the white man, his grandfather's old hunting hatchet. Necessity dictated. Because the land was mined and booby-trapped, it was SOP for each man to carry a steel-centered, nylon-covered flak jacket, which weighed 6.7 pounds, but which on hot days seemed much heavier. Because you could die so quickly, each man carried at least one large compress bandage, usually in the helmet band for easy access. Because the nights were cold, and because the monsoons were wet, each carried a green plastic poncho that could be used as a raincoat or groundsheet or makeshift tent. With its quilted liner, the poncho weighed almost 2 pounds, but it was worth every ounce. In April, for instance, when Ted Lavender was shot, they used his poncho to wrap him up, then to carry him across the paddy, then to lift him into the chopper that took him away.

They were called legs or grunts.

To carry something was to hump it, as when Lieutenant Jimmy Cross humped his love for Martha up the hills and through the swamps. In its intransitive form, to hump meant to walk, or to march, but it implied burdens far beyond the intransitive.

Almost everyone humped photographs. In his wallet, Lieutenant Cross carried two photographs of Martha. The first was a Kodacolor snapshot signed Love, though he knew better. She stood against a brick wall. Her eyes were gray and neutral, her lips slightly open as she stared straight-on at the camera. At night, sometimes, Lieutenant Cross wondered who had taken the picture, because he knew she had boyfriends, because he loved her so much, and because he could see the shadow of the picture-taker spreading out against the brick wall. The second photograph had been clipped from the 1968 Mount Sebastian yearbook. It was an action shot—women's volleyball—and Martha was bent horizontal to the floor, reaching, the palms of her hands in sharp focus, the tongue taut, the expression frank and competitive. There was no visible sweat. She wore white gym shorts. Her legs, he thought, were almost certainly the legs of a virgin, dry and without hair, the left knee cocked and carrying her entire weight, which was just over 117 pounds. Lieutenant Cross remembered touching that left knee. A dark theater, he remembered, and the movie was *Bonnie and Clyde*, and Martha wore a tweed skirt, and during the final scene, when he touched her knee, she turned and looked at him in a sad, sober way that made him pull his hand back, but he would always remember the feel of the tweed skirt and the knee beneath it and the sound of the gunfire that killed Bonnie and Clyde, how embarrassing it was, how slow and oppressive. He remembered kissing her good night at the dorm door. Right then, he thought, he should've done something brave. He should've carried her up the stairs to her room and tied her to the bed and touched that left knee all night long. He should've risked it. Whenever he looked at the photographs, he thought of new things he should've done.

· · ·

What they carried was partly a function of rank, partly of field specialty.

As a first lieutenant and platoon leader, Jimmy Cross carried a compass, maps, code books, binoculars, and a .45-caliber pistol that weighed 2.9 pounds fully loaded. He carried a strobe light and the responsibility for the lives of his men.

As an RTO, Mitchell Sanders carried the PRC-25 radio, a killer, 26 pounds with its battery.

As a medic, Rat Kiley carried a canvas satchel filled with morphine and plasma and malaria tablets and surgical tape and comic books and all the things a medic must carry, including M&M's for especially bad wounds, for a total weight of nearly 18 pounds.

As a big man, therefore a machine gunner, Henry Dobbins carried the M-60, which weighed 23 pounds unloaded, but which was almost always loaded. In addition, Dobbins carried between 10 and 15 pounds of ammunition draped in belts across his chest and shoulders.

As PFCs or Spec 4s, most of them were common grunts and carried the standard M-16 gas-operated assault rifle. The weapon weighed 7.5 pounds unloaded, 8.2 pounds with its full 20-round magazine. Depending on numerous factors, such as topography and psychology, the riflemen carried anywhere from 12 to 20 magazines, usually in cloth bandoliers, adding on another 8.4 pounds at minimum, 14 pounds at maximum. When it was available, they also carried M-16 maintenance gear—rods and steel brushes and swabs and tubes of LSA oil—all of which weighed about a pound. Among the grunts, some carried the M-79 grenade launcher, 5.9 pounds unloaded, a reasonably light weapon except for the ammunition, which was heavy. A single round weighed 10 ounces. The typical load was 25 rounds. But Ted Lavender, who was scared, carried 34 rounds when he was shot and killed outside Than Khe, and he went down under an exceptional burden, more than 20 pounds of ammunition, plus the flak jacket and helmet and rations and water and toilet paper and tranquilizers and all the rest, plus the unweighed fear. He was dead weight. There was no twitching or flopping. Kiowa, who saw it happen, said it was like watching a rock fall, or a big sandbag or something—just boom, then down—not like the movies where the dead guy rolls around and does fancy spins and goes ass over teakettle—not like that, Kiowa said, the poor bastard just flat-fuck fell. Boom. Down. Nothing else. It was a bright morning in mid-April. Lieutenant Cross felt the pain. He blamed himself. They stripped off Lavender's canteens and ammo, all the heavy things, and Rat Kiley said the obvious, the guy's dead, and Mitchell Sanders used his radio to report one U.S. KIA and to request a chopper. Then they wrapped Lavender in his poncho. They carried him out to a dry paddy, established security, and sat smoking the dead man's dope until the chopper came. Lieutenant Cross kept to himself. He pictured Martha's smooth young face, thinking he loved her more than anything, more than his men, and now Ted Lavender was dead because he loved her so much and could not stop thinking about her. When the dustoff arrived, they carried Lavender aboard. Afterward they burned Than Khe. They marched until dusk, then dug their holes, and that night Kiowa kept explaining how you had to be there, how fast it was, how the poor guy just dropped like so much concrete. Boom-down, he said. Like cement.

· · ·

In addition to the three standard weapons—the M-60, M-16, and M-79—they carried whatever presented itself, or whatever seemed appropriate as a means of killing or staying alive. They carried catch-as-catch-can. At various times, in various situations, they carried M-14s and CAR-15s and Swedish Ks and grease guns and captured AK-47s and Chi-Coms and RPGs and Simonov carbines and black market Uzis and .38-caliber Smith & Wesson handguns and 66 mm LAWs and shotguns and silencers and blackjacks and bayonets and C-4 plastic explosives. Lee Strunk carried a slingshot; a weapon of last resort, he called it. Mitchell Sanders carried brass knuckles. Kiowa carried his grandfather's feathered hatchet. Every third or fourth man carried a Claymore antipersonnel mine—3.5 pounds with its firing device. They all carried fragmentation grenades—14 ounces each. They all carried at least one M-18 colored smoke grenade—24 ounces. Some carried CS or tear gas grenades. Some carried white phosphorus grenades. They carried all they could bear, and then some, including a silent awe for the terrible power of the things they carried.

In the first week of April, before Lavender died, Lieutenant Jimmy Cross received a good-luck charm from Martha. It was a simple pebble, an ounce at most. Smooth to the touch, it was a milky white color with flecks of orange and violet, oval-shaped, like a miniature egg. In the accompanying letter, Martha wrote that she had found the pebble on the Jersey shoreline, precisely where the land touched water at high tide, where things came together but also separated. It was this separate-but-together quality, she wrote, that had inspired her to pick up the pebble and to carry it in her breast pocket for several days, where it seemed weightless, and then to send it through the mail, by air, as a token of her truest feelings for him. Lieutenant Cross found this romantic. But he wondered what her truest feelings were, exactly, and what she meant by separate-but-together. He wondered how the tides and waves had come into play on that afternoon along the Jersey shoreline when Martha saw the pebble and bent down to rescue it from geology. He imagined bare feet. Martha was a poet, with the poet's sensibilities, and her feet would be brown and bare, the toenails unpainted, the eyes chilly and somber like the ocean in March, and though it was painful, he wondered who had been with her that afternoon. He imagined a pair of shadows moving along the strip of sand where things came together but also separated. It was phantom jealousy, he knew, but he couldn't help himself. He loved her so much. On the march, through the hot days of early April, he carried the pebble in his mouth, turning it with his tongue, tasting sea salt and moisture. His mind wandered. He had difficulty keeping his attention on the war. On occasion he would yell at his men to spread out the column, to keep their eyes open, but then he would slip away into daydreams, just pretending, walking barefoot along the Jersey shore, with Martha, carrying nothing. He would feel himself rising. Sun and waves and gentle winds, all love and lightness.

What they carried varied by mission.

When a mission took them to the mountains, they carried mosquito netting, machetes, canvas tarps, and extra bug juice.

If a mission seemed especially hazardous, or if it involved

a place they knew to be bad, they carried everything they could. In certain heavily mined AOs, where the land was dense with Toe Poppers and Bouncing Betties, they took turns humping a 28-pound mine detector. With its headphones and big sensing plate, the equipment was a stress on the lower back and shoulders, awkward to handle, often useless because of the shrapnel in the earth, but they carried it anyway, partly for safety, partly for the illusion of safety.

On ambush, or other night missions, they carried peculiar little odds and ends. Kiowa always took along his New Testament and a pair of moccasins for silence. Dave Jensen carried night-sight vitamins high in carotene. Lee Strunk carried his slingshot; ammo, he claimed, would never be a problem. Rat Kiley carried brandy and M&M's candy. Until he was shot, Ted Lavender carried the starlight scope, which weighed 6.3 pounds with its aluminum carrying case. Henry Dobbins carried his girlfriend's pantyhose wrapped around his neck as a comforter. They all carried ghosts. When dark came, they would move out single file across the meadows and paddies to their ambush coordinates, where they would quietly set up the Claymores and lie down and spend the night waiting.

Other missions were more complicated and required special equipment. In mid-April, it was their mission to search out and destroy the elaborate tunnel complexes in the Than Khe area south of Chu Lai. To blow the tunnels, they carried one-pound blocks of pentrite high explosives, four blocks to a man, 68 pounds in all. They carried wiring, detonators, and battery-powered clackers. Dave Jensen carried earplugs. Most often, before blowing the tunnels, they were ordered by higher command to search them, which was considered bad news, but by and large they just shrugged and carried out orders. Because he was a big man, Henry Dobbins was excused from tunnel duty. The others would draw numbers. Before Lavender died there were 17 men in the platoon, and whoever drew the number 17 would strip off his gear and crawl in headfirst with a flashlight and Lieutenant Cross's .45-caliber pistol. The rest of them would fan out as security. They would sit down or kneel, not facing the hole, listening to the ground beneath them, imagining cobwebs and ghosts, whatever was down there—the tunnel walls squeezing in—how the flashlight seemed impossibly heavy in the hand and how it was tunnel vision in the very strictest sense, compression in all ways, even time, and how you had to wiggle in—ass and elbows—a swallowed-up feeling—and how you found yourself worrying about odd things: Will your flashlight go dead? Do rats carry rabies? If you screamed, how far would the sound carry? Would your buddies hear it? Would they have the courage to drag you out? In some respects, though not many, the waiting was worse than the tunnel itself. Imagination was a killer.

On April 16, when Lee Strunk drew the number 17, he laughed and muttered something and went down quickly. The morning was hot and very still. Not good, Kiowa said. He looked at the tunnel opening, then out across a dry paddy toward the village of Than Khe. Nothing moved. No clouds or birds or people. As they waited, the men smoked and drank Kool-Aid, not talking much, feeling sympathy for Lee Strunk but also feeling the luck of the draw. You win some, you lose some, said Mitchell Sanders, and sometimes you settle for a rain check. It was a tired line and no one laughed.

Henry Dobbins ate a tropical chocolate bar. Ted Lavender popped a tranquilizer and went off to pee.

After five minutes, Lieutenant Jimmy Cross moved to the tunnel, leaned down, and examined the darkness. Trouble, he thought—a cave-in maybe. And then suddenly, without willing it, he was thinking about Martha. The stresses and fractures, the quick collapse, the two of them buried alive under all that weight. Dense, crushing love. Kneeling, watching the hole, he tried to concentrate on Lee Strunk and the war, all the dangers, but his love was too much for him, he felt paralyzed, he wanted to sleep inside her lungs and breathe her blood and be smothered. He wanted her to be a virgin and not a virgin, all at once. He wanted to know her. Intimate secrets: Why poetry? Why so sad? Why that grayness in her eyes? Why so alone? Not lonely, just alone—riding her bike across campus or sitting off by herself in the cafeteria—even dancing, she danced alone—and it was the aloneness that filled him with love. He remembered telling her that one evening. How she nodded and looked away. And how, later, when he kissed her, she received the kiss without returning it, her eyes wide open, not afraid, not a virgin's eyes, just flat and uninvolved.

Lieutenant Cross gazed at the tunnel. But he was not there. He was buried with Martha under the white sand at the Jersey shore. They were pressed together, and the pebble in his mouth was her tongue. He was smiling. Vaguely, he was aware of how quiet the day was, the sullen paddies, yet he could not bring himself to worry about matters of security. He was beyond that. He was just a kid at war, in love. He was twenty-four years old. He couldn't help it.

A few moments later Lee Strunk crawled out of the tunnel. He came up grinning, filthy but alive. Lieutenant Cross nodded and closed his eyes while the others clapped Strunk on the back and made jokes about rising from the dead.

Worms, Rat Kiley said. Right out of the grave. Fuckin' zombie.

The men laughed. They all felt great relief.

Spook city, said Mitchell Sanders.

Lee Strunk made a funny ghost sound, a kind of moaning, yet very happy, and right then, when Strunk made that high happy moaning sound, when he went *Ahhooooo*, right then Ted Lavender was shot in the head on his way back from peeing. He lay with his mouth open. The teeth were broken. There was a swollen black bruise under his left eye. The cheekbone was gone. Oh shit, Rat Kiley said, the guy's dead. The guy's dead, he kept saying, which seemed profound—the guy's dead. I mean really.

The things they carried were determined to some extent by superstition. Lieutenant Cross carried his good-luck pebble. Dave Jensen carried a rabbit's foot. Norman Bowker, otherwise a very gentle person, carried a thumb that had been presented to him as a gift by Mitchell Sanders. The thumb was dark brown, rubbery to the touch, and weighed 3 ounces at most. It had been cut from a VC corpse, a boy of fifteen or sixteen. They'd found him at the bottom of an irrigation ditch, badly burned, flies in his mouth and eyes. The boy wore black shorts and sandals. At the time of his death he had been carrying a pouch of rice, a rifle, and three magazines of ammunition.

You want my opinion, Mitchell Sanders said, there's a definite moral here.

He put his hand on the dead boy's wrist. He was quiet for a time, as if counting a pulse, then he patted the stomach, almost affectionately, and used Kiowa's hunting hatchet to remove the thumb.

Henry Dobbins asked what the moral was.

Moral?

You know. *Moral.*

Sanders wrapped the thumb in toilet paper and handed it across to Norman Bowker. There was no blood. Smiling, he kicked the boy's head, watched the flies scatter, and said, It's like with that old TV show—Paladin. Have gun, will travel.

Henry Dobbins thought about it.

Yeah, well, he finally said. I don't see no moral.

There it *is*, man.

Fuck off.


They carried USO stationery and pencils and pens. They carried Sterno, safety pins, trip flares, signal flares, spools of wire, razor blades, chewing tobacco, liberated joss sticks and statuettes of the smiling Buddha, candles, grease pencils, *The Stars and Stripes*, fingernail clippers, Psy Ops leaflets, bush hats, bolos, and much more. Twice a week, when the resupply choppers came in, they carried hot chow in green mermite cans and large canvas bags filled with iced beer and soda pop. They carried plastic water containers, each with a 2-gallon capacity. Mitchell Sanders carried a set of starched tiger fatigues for special occasions. Henry Dobbins carried Black Flag insecticide. Dave Jensen carried empty sandbags that could be filled at night for added protection. Lee Strunk carried tanning lotion. Some things they carried in common.

Taking turns, they carried the big PRC-77 scrambler radio, which weighed 30 pounds with its battery. They shared the weight of memory. They took up what others could no longer bear. Often, they carried each other, the wounded or weak. They carried infections. They carried chess sets, basketballs, Vietnamese-English dictionaries, insignia of rank, Bronze Stars and Purple Hearts, plastic cards imprinted with the Code of Conduct. They carried diseases, among them malaria and dysentery. They carried lice and ringworm and leeches and paddy algae and various rots and molds. They carried the land itself—Vietnam, the place, the soil—a powdery orange-red dust that covered their boots and fatigues and faces. They carried the sky. The whole atmosphere, they carried it, the humidity, the monsoons, the stink of fungus and decay, all of it, they carried gravity. They moved like mules. By daylight they took sniper fire, at night they were mortared, but it was not battle, it was just the endless march, village to village, without purpose, nothing won or lost. They marched for the sake of the march. They plodded along slowly, dumbly, leaning forward against the heat, unthinking, all blood and bone, simple grunts, soldiering with their legs, toiling up the hills and down into the paddies and across the rivers and up again and down, just humping, one step and then the next and then another, but no volition, no will, because it was automatic, it was anatomy, and the war was entirely a matter of posture and carriage, the hump was everything, a kind of inertia, a kind of emptiness, a dullness of desire and intellect and conscience and hope and human sensibility. Their principles were in their feet. Their calculations were biological. They had no sense of strategy or mission. They searched the villages without knowing what to look for, not caring, kicking over jars of rice, frisking children and old men, blowing tunnels, sometimes setting fires and sometimes not, then forming up and moving on to the next village, then other villages, where it would always be the same. They carried their own lives. The pressures were enormous. In the heat of early afternoon, they would remove their helmets and flak jackets, walking bare, which was dangerous but which helped ease the strain. They would often discard things along the route of march. Purely for comfort, they would throw away rations, blow their Claymores and grenades, no matter, because by nightfall the resupply choppers would arrive with more of the same, then a day or two later still more, fresh watermelons and crates of ammunition and sunglasses and woolen sweaters—the resources were stunning—sparklers for the Fourth of July, colored eggs for Easter—it was the great American war chest—the fruits of science, the smokestacks, the canneries, the arsenals at Hartford, the Minnesota forests, the machine shops, the vast fields of corn and wheat—they carried like freight trains; they carried it on their backs and shoulders—and for all the ambiguities of Vietnam, all the mysteries and unknowns, there was at least the single abiding certainty that they would never be at a loss for things to carry.

After the chopper took Lavender away, Lieutenant Jimmy Cross led his men into the village of Than Khe. They burned everything. They shot chickens and dogs, they trashed the village well, they called in artillery and watched the wreckage, then they marched for several hours through the hot afternoon, and then at dusk, while Kiowa explained how Lavender died, Lieutenant Cross found himself trembling.

He tried not to cry. With his entrenching tool, which weighed 5 pounds, he began digging a hole in the earth.

He felt shame. He hated himself. He had loved Martha more than his men, and as a consequence Lavender was now dead, and this was something he would have to carry like a stone in his stomach for the rest of the war.

All he could do was dig. He used his entrenching tool like an ax, slashing, feeling both love and hate, and then later, when it was full dark, he sat at the bottom of his foxhole and wept. It went on for a long while. In part, he was grieving for Ted Lavender, but mostly it was for Martha, and for himself, because she belonged to another world, which was not quite real, and because she was a junior at Mount Sebastian College in New Jersey, a poet and a virgin and uninvolved, and because he realized she did not love him and never would.

Like cement, Kiowa whispered in the dark. I swear to God—boom, down. Not a word.

I've heard this, said Norman Bowker.

A pisser, you know? Still zipping himself up. Zapped while zipping.

All right, fine. That's enough.

Yeah, but you had to see it, the guy just—

I *heard*, man. Cement. So why not shut the fuck *up*?

Kiowa shook his head sadly and glanced over at the hole where Lieutenant Jimmy Cross sat watching the night. The air was thick and wet. A warm dense fog had settled over the paddies and there was the stillness that precedes rain.

After a time Kiowa sighed.

One thing for sure, he said. The lieutenant's in some deep hurt. I mean that crying jag—the way he was carrying on—it wasn't fake or anything, it was real heavy-duty hurt. The man cares.

Sure, Norman Bowker said.

Say what you want, the man does care.

We all got problems.

Not Lavender.

No, I guess not, Bowker said. Do me a favor, though.

Shut up?

That's a smart Indian. Shut up.

Shrugging, Kiowa pulled off his boots. He wanted to say more, just to lighten up his sleep, but instead he opened his New Testament and arranged it beneath his head as a pillow. The fog made things seem hollow and unattached. He tried not to think about Ted Lavender, but then he was thinking how fast it was, no drama, down and dead, and how it was hard to feel anything except surprise. It seemed unchristian. He wished he could find some great sadness, or even anger, but the emotion wasn't there and he couldn't make it happen. Mostly he felt pleased to be alive. He liked the smell of the New Testament under his cheek, the leather and ink and paper and glue, whatever the chemicals were. He liked hearing the sounds of night. Even his fatigue, it felt fine, the stiff muscles and the prickly awareness of his own body, a floating feeling. He enjoyed not being dead. Lying there, Kiowa admired Lieutenant Jimmy Cross's capacity for grief. He wanted to share the man's pain, he wanted to care as Jimmy Cross cared. And yet when he closed his eyes, all he could think was Boom-down, and all he could feel was the plea-

sure of having his boots off and the fog curling in around
him and the damp soil and the Bible smells and the plush
comfort of night.

After a moment Norman Bowker sat up in the dark.

What the hell, he said. You want to talk, *talk*. Tell it to
me.

Forget it.

No, man, go on. One thing I hate, it's a silent Indian.


For the most part they carried themselves with poise, a
kind of dignity. Now and then, however, there were times of
panic, when they squealed or wanted to squeal but couldn't,
when they twitched and made moaning sounds and covered their heads and said Dear Jesus and flopped around on
the earth and fired their weapons blindly and cringed and
sobbed and begged for the noise to stop and went wild and
made stupid promises to themselves and to God and to their
mothers and fathers, hoping not to die. In different ways, it
happened to all of them. Afterward, when the firing ended,
they would blink and peek up. They would touch their bodies, feeling shame, then quickly hiding it. They would force
themselves to stand. As if in slow motion, frame by frame,
the world would take on the old logic—absolute silence,
then the wind, then sunlight, then voices. It was the burden of being alive. Awkwardly, the men would reassemble
themselves, first in private, then in groups, becoming soldiers
again. They would repair the leaks in their eyes. They would
check for casualties, call in dustoffs, light cigarettes, try to
smile, clear their throats and spit and begin cleaning their
weapons. After a time someone would shake his head and
say, No lie, I almost shit my pants, and someone else would

laugh, which meant it was bad, yes, but the guy had obviously not shit his pants, it wasn't that bad, and in any case nobody would ever do such a thing and then go ahead and talk about it. They would squint into the dense, oppressive sunlight. For a few moments, perhaps, they would fall silent, lighting a joint and tracking its passage from man to man, inhaling, holding in the humiliation. Scary stuff, one of them might say. But then someone else would grin or flick his eyebrows and say, Roger-dodger, almost cut me a new asshole, *almost.*

There were numerous such poses. Some carried themselves with a sort of wistful resignation, others with pride or stiff soldierly discipline or good humor or macho zeal. They were afraid of dying but they were even more afraid to show it.

They found jokes to tell.

They used a hard vocabulary to contain the terrible softness. *Greased* they'd say. *Offed, lit up, zapped while zipping.* It wasn't cruelty, just stage presence. They were actors. When someone died, it wasn't quite dying, because in a curious way it seemed scripted, and because they had their lines mostly memorized, irony mixed with tragedy, and because they called it by other names, as if to encyst and destroy the reality of death itself. They kicked corpses. They cut off thumbs. They talked grunt lingo. They told stories about Ted Lavender's supply of tranquilizers, how the poor guy didn't feel a thing, how incredibly tranquil he was.

There's a moral here, said Mitchell Sanders.

They were waiting for Lavender's chopper, smoking the dead man's dope.

The moral's pretty obvious, Sanders said, and winked.

Stay away from drugs. No joke, they'll ruin your day every time.

Cute, said Henry Dobbins.

Mind blower, get it? Talk about wiggy. Nothing left, just blood and brains.

They made themselves laugh.

There it is, they'd say. Over and over—there it is, my friend, there it is—as if the repetition itself were an act of poise, a balance between crazy and almost crazy, knowing without going, there it is, which meant be cool, let it ride, because Oh yeah, man, you can't change what can't be changed, there it is, there it absolutely and positively and fucking well *is*.

They were tough.

They carried all the emotional baggage of men who might die. Grief, terror, love, longing—these were intangibles, but the intangibles had their own mass and specific gravity, they had tangible weight. They carried shameful memories. They carried the common secret of cowardice barely restrained, the instinct to run or freeze or hide, and in many respects this was the heaviest burden of all, for it could never be put down, it required perfect balance and perfect posture. They carried their reputations. They carried the soldier's greatest fear, which was the fear of blushing. Men killed, and died, because they were embarrassed not to. It was what had brought them to the war in the first place, nothing positive, no dreams of glory or honor, just to avoid the blush of dishonor. They died so as not to die of embarrassment. They crawled into tunnels and walked point and advanced under fire. Each morning, despite the unknowns, they made their legs move. They endured. They kept humping. They did not submit to the obvious alternative, which was simply to close the eyes and fall. So easy, really. Go limp and tumble to the ground and let the muscles unwind and not speak and not budge until your buddies picked you up and lifted you into the chopper that would roar and dip its nose and carry you off to the world. A mere matter of falling, yet no one ever fell. It was not courage, exactly; the object was not valor. Rather, they were too frightened to be cowards.

By and large they carried these things inside, maintaining the masks of composure. They sneered at sick call. They spoke bitterly about guys who had found release by shooting off their own toes or fingers. Pussies, they'd say. Candy-asses. It was fierce, mocking talk, with only a trace of envy or awe, but even so the image played itself out behind their eyes.

They imagined the muzzle against flesh. So easy: squeeze the trigger and blow away a toe. They imagined it. They imagined the quick, sweet pain, then the evacuation to Japan, then a hospital with warm beds and cute geisha nurses.

And they dreamed of freedom birds.

At night, on guard, staring into the dark, they were carried away by jumbo jets. They felt the rush of takeoff. Gone! they yelled. And then velocity—wings and engines—a smiling stewardess—but it was more than a plane, it was a real bird, a big sleek silver bird with feathers and talons and high screeching. They were flying. The weights fell off; there was nothing to bear. They laughed and held on tight, feeling the cold slap of wind and altitude, soaring, thinking *It's over, I'm gone!*—they were naked, they were light and free—it was all lightness, bright and fast and buoyant, light as light, a helium buzz in the brain, a giddy bubbling in the lungs as they were taken up over the clouds and the war, beyond duty, beyond gravity and mortification and global entanglements— *Sin loi!*, they yelled. *I'm sorry, motherfuckers, but I'm out of it, I'm goofed, I'm on a space cruise, I'm gone!*—and it was a restful, unencumbered sensation, just riding the light waves, sailing that big silver freedom bird over the mountains and oceans, over America, over the farms and great sleeping cities and cemeteries and highways and the golden arches of McDonald's, it was flight, a kind of fleeing, a kind of falling, falling higher and higher, spinning off the edge of the earth and beyond the sun and through the vast, silent vacuum where there were no burdens and where everything weighed exactly nothing— *Gone!* they screamed. *I'm sorry but I'm gone!*—and so at night, not quite dreaming, they gave themselves over to lightness, they were carried, they were purely borne.

On the morning after Ted Lavender died, First Lieutenant Jimmy Cross crouched at the bottom of his foxhole and burned Martha's letters. Then he burned the two photographs. There was a steady rain falling, which made it difficult, but he used heat tabs and Sterno to build a small fire, screening it with his body, holding the photographs over the tight blue flame with the tips of his fingers.

He realized it was only a gesture. Stupid, he thought. Sentimental, too, but mostly just stupid.

Lavender was dead. You couldn't burn the blame.

Besides, the letters were in his head. And even now, without photographs, Lieutenant Cross could see Martha playing volleyball in her white gym shorts and yellow T-shirt. He could see her moving in the rain.

When the fire died out, Lieutenant Cross pulled his poncho over his shoulders and ate breakfast from a can.

There was no great mystery, he decided.

In those burned letters Martha had never mentioned the war, except to say, Jimmy, take care of yourself. She wasn't involved. She signed the letters Love, but it wasn't love, and all the fine lines and technicalities did not matter. Virginity was no longer an issue. He hated her. Yes, he did. He hated her. Love, too, but it was a hard, hating kind of love.

The morning came up wet and blurry. Everything seemed part of everything else, the fog and Martha and the deepening rain.

He was a soldier, after all.

Half smiling, Lieutenant Jimmy Cross took out his maps. He shook his head hard, as if to clear it, then bent forward and began planning the day's march. In ten minutes, or maybe twenty, he would rouse the men and they would pack up and head west, where the maps showed the country to be green and inviting. They would do what they had always done. The rain might add some weight, but otherwise it would be one more day layered upon all the other days.

He was realistic about it. There was that new hardness in his stomach. He loved her but he hated her.

No more fantasies, he told himself.

Henceforth, when he thought about Martha, it would be only to think that she belonged elsewhere. He would shut down the daydreams. This was not Mount Sebastian, it was another world, where there were no pretty poems or midterm exams, a place where men died because of carelessness and gross stupidity. Kiowa was right. Boom-down, and you were dead, never partly dead.

Briefly, in the rain, Lieutenant Cross saw Martha's gray eyes gazing back at him.

He understood.

It was very sad, he thought. The things men carried inside. The things men did or felt they had to do.

He almost nodded at her, but didn't.

Instead he went back to his maps. He was now determined to perform his duties firmly and without negligence. It wouldn't help Lavender, he knew that, but from this point on he would comport himself as an officer. He would dispose of his good-luck pebble. Swallow it, maybe, or use Lee Strunk's slingshot, or just drop it along the trail. On the march he would impose strict field discipline. He would be careful to send out flank security, to prevent straggling or bunching up, to keep his troops moving at the proper pace and at the proper interval. He would insist on clean weapons. He would confiscate the remainder of Lavender's dope. Later in the day, perhaps, he would call the men together and speak to them plainly. He would accept the blame for what had happened to Ted Lavender. He would be a man about it. He would look them in the eyes, keeping his chin level, and he would issue the new SOPs in a calm, impersonal tone of voice, a lieutenant's voice, leaving no room for argument or discussion. Commencing immediately, he'd tell them, they would no longer abandon equipment along the route of march. They would police up their acts. They would get their shit together, and keep it together, and maintain it neatly and in good working order.

He would not tolerate laxity. He would show strength, distancing himself.

Among the men there would be grumbling, of course,

and maybe worse, because their days would seem longer and their loads heavier, but Lieutenant Jimmy Cross reminded himself that his obligation was not to be loved but to lead. He would dispense with love; it was not now a factor. And if anyone quarreled or complained, he would simply tighten his lips and arrange his shoulders in the correct command posture. He might give a curt little nod. Or he might not. He might just shrug and say, Carry on, then they would saddle up and form into a column and move out toward the villages west of Than Khe.

# Love

Many years after the war Jimmy Cross came to visit me at my home in Massachusetts, and for a full day we drank coffee and smoked cigarettes and talked about everything we had seen and done so long ago, all the things we still carried through our lives. Spread out across the kitchen table were maybe a hundred old photographs. There were pictures of Rat Kiley and Kiowa and Mitchell Sanders, all of us, the faces incredibly soft and young. At one point, I remember, we paused over a snapshot of Ted Lavender, and after a while Jimmy rubbed his eyes and said he'd never forgiven himself for Lavender's death. It was something that would never go away, he said quietly, and I nodded and told him I felt the same about certain things. Then for a long time neither of us could think of much to say. The thing to do, we decided, was to forget the coffee and switch to gin, which improved the mood, and not much later we were laughing about some of the craziness that used to go on. The way Henry Dobbins carried his girl-friend's pantyhose around his neck like a comforter. Kiowa's moccasins and hunting hatchet. Rat Kiley's comic books. By midnight we were both a little high, and I decided there was no harm in asking about Martha. I'm not sure how I phrased it—just a general question—but Jimmy Cross looked up in surprise. "You writer types," he said, "you've got long memories." Then he smiled and excused himself and went up to the guest room and came back with a small framed photograph. It was the volleyball shot: Martha bent horizontal to the floor, reaching, the palms of her hands in sharp focus.

"Remember this?" he said.

I nodded and told him I was surprised. I thought he'd burned it.

Jimmy kept smiling. For a while he stared down at the photograph, his eyes very bright, then he shrugged and said, "Well, I did—I burned it. After Lavender died, I couldn't . . . This is a new one. Martha gave it to me herself."

They'd run into each other, he said, at a college reunion in 1979. Nothing had changed. He still loved her. For eight or nine hours, he said, they spent most of their time together. There was a banquet, and then a dance, and then afterward they took a walk across the campus and talked about their lives. Martha was a Lutheran missionary now. A trained nurse, although nursing wasn't the point, and she had done service in Ethiopia and Guatemala and Mexico. She had never married, she said, and probably never would. She didn't know why. But as she said this, her eyes seemed to slide sideways, and it occurred to him that there were things about her he would never know. Her eyes were

gray and neutral. Later, when he took her hand, there was
no pressure in return, and later still, when he told her he
still loved her, she kept walking and didn't answer and then
after several minutes looked at her wristwatch and said it
was getting late. He walked her back to the dormitory. For a
few moments he considered asking her to his room, but instead he laughed and told her how back in college he'd almost done something very brave. It was after seeing *Bonnie
and Clyde*, he said, and on this same spot he'd almost picked
her up and carried her to his room and tied her to the bed
and put his hand on her knee and just held it there all night
long. It came close, he told her—he'd almost done it. Martha shut her eyes. She crossed her arms at her chest, as if
suddenly cold, rocking slightly, then after a time she looked
at him and said she was glad he hadn't tried it. She didn't
understand how men could do those things. What things? he
asked, and Martha said, The things men do. Then he nodded. It began to form. Oh, he said, those things. At breakfast
the next morning she told him she was sorry. She explained
that there was nothing she could do about it, and he said he
understood, and then she laughed and gave him the picture
and told him not to burn this one up.

Jimmy shook his head. "It doesn't matter," he finally said.
"I love her."

For the rest of his visit I steered the conversation away
from Martha. At the end, though, as we were walking out to
his car, I told him that I'd like to write a story about some of
this. Jimmy thought it over and then gave me a little smile.
"Why not?" he said. "Maybe she'll read it and come begging.
There's always hope, right?"

"Right," I said.

He got into his car and rolled down the window. "Make me out to be a good guy, okay? Brave and handsome, all that stuff. Best platoon leader ever." He hesitated for a second. "And do me a favor. Don't mention anything about—"

"No," I said, "I won't."

# Spin

The war wasn't all terror and violence. Sometimes things could almost get sweet. For instance, I remember a little boy with a plastic leg. I remember how he hopped over to Azar and asked for a chocolate bar— "GI number one," the kid said—and Azar laughed and handed over the chocolate. When the boy hopped away, Azar clucked his tongue and said, "War's a bitch." He shook his head sadly. "One leg, for Chrissake. Some poor fucker ran out of ammo."

I remember Mitchell Sanders sitting quietly in the shade of an old banyan tree. He was using a thumbnail to pry off the body lice, working slowly, carefully depositing the lice in a blue USO envelope. His eyes were tired. It had been a long two weeks in the bush. After an hour or so he sealed up the envelope, wrote FREE in the upper right-hand corner, and addressed it to his draft board in Ohio.

On occasions the war was like a Ping-Pong ball. You could put fancy spin on it, you could make it dance.

I remember Norman Bowker and Henry Dobbins playing checkers every evening before dark. It was a ritual for them. They would dig a foxhole and get the board out and play long, silent games as the sky went from pink to purple. The rest of us would sometimes stop by to watch. There was something restful about it, something orderly and reassuring. There were red checkers and black checkers. The playing field was laid out in a strict grid, no tunnels or mountains or jungles. You knew where you stood. You knew the score. The pieces were out on the board, the enemy was visible, you could watch the tactics unfolding into larger strategies. There was a winner and a loser. There were rules.

I'm forty-three years old, and a writer now, and the war has been over for a long while. Much of it is hard to remember. I sit at this typewriter and stare through my words and watch Kiowa sinking into the deep muck of a shit field, or Curt Lemon hanging in pieces from a tree, and as I write about these things, the remembering is turned into a kind of rehappening. Kiowa yells at me. Curt Lemon steps from the shade into bright sunlight, his face brown and shining, and then he soars into a tree. The bad stuff never stops happening: it lives in its own dimension, replaying itself over and over.

But the war wasn't all that way.

Like when Ted Lavender went too heavy on the tranquilizers. "How's the war today?" somebody would say, and Ted

Lavender would give a soft, spacey smile and say, "Mellow, man. We got ourselves a nice mellow war today."

And like the time we enlisted an old poppa-san to guide us through the mine fields out on the Batangan Peninsula. The old guy walked with a limp, slow and stooped over, but he knew where the safe spots were and where you had to be careful and where even if you were careful you could end up like popcorn. He had a tightrope walker's feel for the land beneath him—its surface tension, the give and take of things. Each morning we'd form up in a long column, the old poppa-san out front, and for the whole day we'd troop along after him, tracing his footsteps, playing an exact and ruthless game of follow the leader. Rat Kiley made up a rhyme that caught on, and we'd all be chanting it together: *Step out of line, hit a mine; follow the dink, you're in the pink.* All around us, the place was littered with Bouncing Betties and Toe Poppers and booby-trapped artillery rounds, but in those five days on the Batangan Peninsula nobody got hurt. We all learned to love the old man.

It was a sad scene when the choppers came to take us away. Jimmy Cross gave the old poppa-san a hug. Mitchell Sanders and Lee Strunk loaded him up with boxes of C rations.

There were actually tears in the old guy's eyes. "Follow dink," he said to each of us, "you go pink."

If you weren't humping, you were waiting. I remember the monotony. Digging foxholes. Slapping mosquitoes. The sun and the heat and the endless paddies. Even in the deep bush, where you could die any number of ways, the war was nakedly and aggressively boring. But it was a strange boredom. It was boredom with a twist, the kind of boredom that caused stomach disorders. You'd be sitting at the top of a high hill, the flat paddies stretching out below, and the day would be calm and hot and utterly vacant, and you'd feel the boredom dripping inside you like a leaky faucet, except it wasn't water, it was a sort of acid, and with each little droplet you'd feel the stuff eating away at important organs. You'd try to relax. You'd uncurl your fists and let your thoughts go. Well, you'd think, this isn't so bad. And right then you'd hear gunfire behind you and your nuts would fly up into your throat and you'd be squealing pig squeals. That kind of boredom.

I feel guilty sometimes. Forty-three years old and I'm still writing war stories. My daughter Kathleen tells me it's an obsession, that I should write about a little girl who finds a million dollars and spends it all on a Shetland pony. In a way, I guess, she's right: I should forget it. But the thing about remembering is that you don't forget. You take your material where you find it, which is in your life, at the intersection of past and present. The memory-traffic feeds into a rotary up on your head, where it goes in circles for a while, then pretty soon imagination flows in and the traffic merges and shoots off down a thousand different streets. As a writer, all you can do is pick a street and go for the ride, putting things down as they come at you. That's the real obsession. All those stories.

Not bloody stories, necessarily. Happy stories, too, and even a few peace stories.

• • •

Here's a quick peace story:

A guy goes AWOL. Shacks up in Danang with a Red Cross nurse. It's a great time — the nurse loves him to death — the guy gets whatever he wants whenever he wants it. The war's over, he thinks. Just nookie and new angles. But then one day he rejoins his unit in the bush. Can't wait to get back into action. Finally one of his buddies asks what happened with the nurse, why so hot for combat, and the guy says, "All that peace, man, it felt so good it hurt. I want to hurt it *back*."

I remember Mitchell Sanders smiling as he told me that story. Most of it he made up, I'm sure, but even so it gave me a quick truth-goose. Because it's all relative. You're pinned down in some filthy hellhole of a paddy, getting your ass delivered to kingdom come, but then for a few seconds everything goes quiet and you look up and see the sun and a few puffy white clouds, and the immense serenity flashes against your eyeballs — the whole world gets rearranged — and even though you're pinned down by a war you never felt more at peace.

What sticks to memory, often, are those odd little fragments that have no beginning and no end:

Norman Bowker lying on his back one night, watching the stars, then whispering to me, "I'll tell you something, O'Brien. If I could have one wish, anything, I'd wish for my dad to write me a letter and say it's okay if I don't win any medals. That's all my old man talks about, nothing else. How he can't wait to see my goddamn medals."

• • •

Or Kiowa teaching a rain dance to Rat Kiley and Dave Jensen, the three of them whooping and leaping around barefoot while a bunch of villagers looked on with a mixture of fascination and giggly horror. Afterward, Rat said, "So where's the rain?" and Kiowa said, "The earth is slow, but the buffalo is patient," and Rat thought about it and said, "Yeah, but where's the *rain?*"

Or Ted Lavender adopting an orphan puppy — feeding it from a plastic spoon and carrying it in his rucksack until the day Azar strapped the puppy to a Claymore antipersonnel mine and squeezed the firing device.

The average age in our platoon, I'd guess, was nineteen or twenty, and as a consequence things often took on a curiously playful atmosphere, like a sporting event at some exotic reform school. The competition could be lethal, yet there was a childlike exuberance to it all, lots of pranks and horseplay. Like when Azar blew away Ted Lavender's puppy. "What's everybody so upset about?" Azar said. "I mean, Christ, I'm just a *boy.*"

I remember these things, too.

The damp, fungal scent of an empty body bag.

A quarter moon rising over the nighttime paddies.

Henry Dobbins sitting in the twilight, sewing on his new buck-sergeant stripes, quietly singing, "A tisket, a tasket, a green and yellow basket."

A field of elephant grass weighted with wind, bowing under the stir of a helicopter's blades, the grass dark and servile, bending low, but then rising straight again when the chopper went away.

A red clay trail outside the village of My Khe.

A hand grenade.

A slim, dead, dainty young man of about twenty.

Kiowa saying, "No choice, Tim. What else could you do?"

Kiowa saying, "Right?"

Kiowa saying, "Talk to me."

Forty-three years old, and the war occurred half a lifetime ago, and yet the remembering makes it now. And sometimes remembering will lead to a story, which makes it forever. That's what stories are for. Stories are for joining the past to the future. Stories are for those late hours in the night when you can't remember how you got from where you were to where you are. Stories are for eternity, when memory is erased, when there is nothing to remember except the story.

# On the Rainy River

This is one story I've never told before. Not to anyone. Not to my parents, not to my brother or sister, not even to my wife. To go into it, I've always thought, would only cause embarrassment for all of us, a sudden need to be elsewhere, which is the natural response to a confession. Even now, I'll admit, the story makes me squirm. For more than twenty years I've had to live with it, feeling the shame, trying to push it away, and so by this act of remembrance, by putting the facts down on paper, I'm hoping to relieve at least some of the pressure on my dreams. Still, it's a hard story to tell. All of us, I suppose, like to believe that in a moral emergency we will behave like the heroes of our youth, bravely and forthrightly, without thought of personal loss or discredit. Certainly that was my conviction back in the summer of 1968. Tim O'Brien: a secret hero. The Lone Ranger. If the stakes ever became high enough—if the evil were evil enough, if the good were good enough—I would simply tap a secret reservoir of courage that had been accumulating inside me over the years. Courage, I seemed to think, comes to us in finite quantities, like an inheritance, and by being frugal and stashing it away and letting it earn interest, we steadily increase our moral capital in preparation for that day when the account must be drawn down. It was a comforting theory. It dispensed with all those bothersome little acts of daily courage; it offered hope and grace to the repetitive coward; it justified the past while amortizing the future.

In June of 1968, a month after graduating from Macalester College, I was drafted to fight a war I hated. I was twenty-one years old. Young, yes, and politically naive, but even so the American war in Vietnam seemed to me wrong. Certain blood was being shed for uncertain reasons. I saw no unity of purpose, no consensus on matters of philosophy or history or law. The very facts were shrouded in uncertainty: Was it a civil war? A war of national liberation or simple aggression? Who started it, and when, and why? What really happened to the USS *Maddox* on that dark night in the Gulf of Tonkin? Was Ho Chi Minh a Communist stooge, or a nationalist savior, or both, or neither? What about the Geneva Accords? What about SEATO and the Cold War? What about dominoes? America was divided on these and a thousand other issues, and the debate had spilled out across the floor of the United States Senate and into the streets, and smart men in pinstripes could not agree on even the most fundamental matters of public policy. The only certainty that summer was moral confusion. It was my view then, and still is, that you don't make war without knowing why. Knowledge, of course, is always imperfect, but it seemed to me that when a nation goes to war it must have reasonable confidence in the justice and imperative of its cause. You can't fix your mistakes. Once people are dead, you can't make them undead.

In any case those were my convictions, and back in college I had taken a modest stand against the war. Nothing radical, no hothead stuff, just ringing a few doorbells for Gene McCarthy, composing a few tedious, uninspired editorials for the campus newspaper. Oddly, though, it was almost entirely an intellectual activity. I brought some energy to it, of course, but it was the energy that accompanies almost any abstract endeavor; I felt no personal danger; I felt no sense of an impending crisis in my life. Stupidly, with a kind of smug removal that I can't begin to fathom, I assumed that the problems of killing and dying did not fall within my special province.

The draft notice arrived on June 17, 1968. It was a humid afternoon, I remember, cloudy and very quiet, and I'd just come in from a round of golf. My mother and father were having lunch out in the kitchen. I remember opening up the letter, scanning the first few lines, feeling the blood go thick behind my eyes. I remember a sound in my head. It wasn't thinking, just a silent howl. A million things all at once—I was too *good* for this war. Too smart, too compassionate, too everything. It couldn't happen. I was above it. I had the world dicked—Phi Beta Kappa and summa cum laude and president of the student body and a full-ride scholarship for grad studies at Harvard. A mistake, maybe—a foul-up in the paperwork. I was no soldier. I hated Boy Scouts. I hated camping out. I hated dirt and tents and mosquitoes. The sight of blood made me queasy, and I couldn't tolerate authority, and I didn't know a rifle from a slingshot. I was a *liberal*, for Christ sake: If they needed fresh bodies, why not draft some back-to-the-stone-age hawk? Or some dumb jingo in his hard hat and Bomb Hanoi button, or one of LBJ's pretty daughters, or Westmoreland's whole handsome family—nephews and nieces and baby grandson. There should be a law, I thought. If you support a war, if you think it's worth the price, that's fine, but you have to put your own precious fluids on the line. You have to head for the front and hook up with an infantry unit and help spill the blood. And you have to bring along your wife, or your kids, or your lover. A *law*, I thought.

I remember the rage in my stomach. Later it burned down to a smoldering self-pity, then to numbness. At dinner that night my father asked what my plans were. "Nothing," I said. "Wait."

I spent the summer of 1968 working in an Armour meat-packing plant in my hometown of Worthington, Minnesota. The plant specialized in pork products, and for eight hours a day I stood on a quarter-mile assembly line—more properly, a disassembly line—removing blood clots from the necks of dead pigs. My job title, I believe, was Declotter. After slaughter, the hogs were decapitated, split down the length of the belly, pried open, eviscerated, and strung up by the hind hocks on a high conveyer belt. Then gravity took over. By the time a carcass reached my spot on the line, the fluids had mostly drained out, everything except for dense clots of blood in the neck and upper chest cavity. To remove the stuff, I used a kind of water gun. The machine was heavy, maybe eighty pounds, and was suspended from the ceiling by a thick rubber cord. There was some bounce to it, an elastic up-and-down give, and the trick was to maneuver the gun with your whole body, not lifting with the arms, just letting the rubber cord do the work for you. At one end was a trigger; at the muzzle end was a small nozzle and a steel roller brush. As a carcass passed by, you'd lean forward and swing the gun up against the clots and squeeze the trigger, all in one motion, and the brush would whirl and water would come shooting out and you'd hear a quick splattering sound as the clots dissolved into a fine red mist. It was not pleasant work. Goggles were a necessity, and a rubber apron, but even so it was like standing for eight hours a day under a lukewarm blood-shower. At night I'd go home smelling of pig. It wouldn't go away. Even after a hot bath, scrubbing hard, the stink was always there—like old bacon, or sausage, a greasy pig-stink that soaked deep into my skin and hair. Among other things, I remember, it was tough getting dates that summer. I felt isolated; I spent a lot of time alone. And there was also that draft notice tucked away in my wallet.

In the evenings I'd sometimes borrow my father's car and drive aimlessly around town, feeling sorry for myself, thinking about the war and the pig factory and how my life seemed to be collapsing toward slaughter. I felt paralyzed. All around me the options seemed to be narrowing, as if I were hurtling down a huge black funnel, the whole world squeezing in tight. There was no happy way out. The government had ended most graduate school deferments; the waiting lists for the National Guard and Reserves were impossibly long; my health was solid; I didn't qualify for CO status—no religious grounds, no history as a pacifist. Moreover, I could not claim to be opposed to war as a matter of general principle.

There were occasions, I believed, when a nation was justified in using military force to achieve its ends, to stop a Hitler or some comparable evil, and I told myself that in such circumstances I would've willingly marched off to the battle. The problem, though, was that a draft board did not let you choose your war.

Beyond all this, or at the very center, was the raw fact of terror. I did not want to die. Not ever. But certainly not then, not there, not in a wrong war. Driving up Main Street, past the courthouse and the Ben Franklin store, I sometimes felt the fear spreading inside me like weeds. I imagined myself dead. I imagined myself doing things I could not do — charging an enemy position, taking aim at another human being.

At some point in mid-July I began thinking seriously about Canada. The border lay a few hundred miles north, an eight-hour drive. Both my conscience and my instincts were telling me to make a break for it, just take off and run like hell and never stop. In the beginning the idea seemed purely abstract, the word Canada printing itself out in my head; but after a time I could see particular shapes and images, the sorry details of my own future — a hotel room in Winnipeg, a battered old suitcase, my father's eyes as I tried to explain myself over the telephone. I could almost hear his voice, and my mother's. Run, I'd think. Then I'd think, Impossible. Then a second later I'd think, *Run*.

It was a moral split. I couldn't make up my mind. I feared the war, yes, but I also feared exile. I was afraid of walking away from my own life, my friends and my family, my whole history, everything that mattered to me. I feared losing the respect of my parents. I feared the law. I feared ridicule and censure. My hometown was a conservative little spot on the prairie, a place where tradition counted, and it was easy to imagine people sitting around a table down at the old Gobbler Café on Main Street, coffee cups poised, the conversation slowly zeroing in on the young O'Brien kid, how the damned sissy had taken off for Canada. At night, when I couldn't sleep, I'd sometimes carry on fierce arguments with those people. I'd be screaming at them, telling them how much I detested their blind, thoughtless, automatic acquiescence to it all, their simpleminded patriotism, their prideful ignorance, their love-it-or-leave-it platitudes, how they were sending me off to fight a war they didn't understand and didn't want to understand. I held them responsible. By God, yes, I *did*. All of them—I held them personally and individually responsible—the polyestered Kiwanis boys, the merchants and farmers, the pious churchgoers, the chatty housewives, the PTA and the Lions club and the Veterans of Foreign Wars and the fine upstanding gentry out at the country club. They didn't know Bao Dai from the man in the moon. They didn't know history. They didn't know the first thing about Diem's tyranny, or the nature of Vietnamese nationalism, or the long colonialism of the French—this was all too damned complicated, it required some reading—but no matter, it was a war to stop the Communists, plain and simple, which was how they liked things, and you were a treasonous pussy if you had second thoughts about killing or dying for plain and simple reasons.

I was bitter, sure. But it was so much more than that. The emotions went from outrage to terror to bewilderment to guilt to sorrow and then back again to outrage. I felt a sickness inside me. Real disease.

Most of this I've told before, or at least hinted at, but

what I have never told is the full truth. How I cracked. How at work one morning, standing on the pig line, I felt something break open in my chest. I don't know what it was. I'll never know. But it was real, I know that much, it was a physical rupture—a cracking-leaking-popping feeling. I remember dropping my water gun. Quickly, almost without thought, I took off my apron and walked out of the plant and drove home. It was midmorning, I remember, and the house was empty. Down in my chest there was still that leaking sensation, something very warm and precious spilling out, and I was covered with blood and hog-stink, and for a long while I just concentrated on holding myself together. I remember taking a hot shower. I remember packing a suitcase and carrying it out to the kitchen, standing very still for a few minutes, looking carefully at the familiar objects all around me. The old chrome toaster, the telephone, the pink and white Formica on the kitchen counters. The room was full of bright sunshine. Everything sparkled. My house, I thought. My life. I'm not sure how long I stood there, but later I scribbled out a short note to my parents.

What it said, exactly, I don't recall now. Something vague. Taking off, will call, love Tim.

I drove north.

It's a blur now, as it was then, and all I remember is velocity and the feel of a steering wheel in my hands. I was riding on adrenaline. A giddy feeling, in a way, except there was the dreamy edge of impossibility to it—like running a dead-end maze—no way out—it couldn't come to a happy conclusion and yet I was doing it anyway because it was all I could think of to do. It was pure flight, fast and mindless.

I had no plan. Just hit the border at high speed and crash through and keep on running. Near dusk I passed through Bemidji, then turned northeast toward International Falls. I spent the night in the car behind a closed-down gas station a half mile from the border. In the morning, after gassing up, I headed straight west along the Rainy River, which separates Minnesota from Canada, and which for me separated one life from another. The land was mostly wilderness. Here and there I passed a motel or bait shop, but otherwise the country unfolded in great sweeps of pine and birch and sumac. Though it was still August, the air already had the smell of October, football season, piles of yellow-red leaves, everything crisp and clean. I remember a huge blue sky. Off to my right was the Rainy River, wide as a lake in places, and beyond the Rainy River was Canada.

For a while I just drove, not aiming at anything, then in the late morning I began looking for a place to lie low for a day or two. I was exhausted, and scared sick, and around noon I pulled into an old fishing resort called the Tip Top Lodge. Actually it was not a lodge at all, just eight or nine tiny yellow cabins clustered on a peninsula that jutted northward into the Rainy River. The place was in sorry shape. There was a dangerous wooden dock, an old minnow tank, a flimsy tar paper boathouse along the shore. The main building, which stood in a cluster of pines on high ground, seemed to lean heavily to one side, like a cripple, the roof sagging toward Canada. Briefly, I thought about turning around, just giving up, but then I got out of the car and walked up to the front porch.

The man who opened the door that day is the hero of my life. How do I say this without sounding sappy? Blurt it out—the man saved me. He offered exactly what I needed, without questions, without any words at all. He took me in. He was there at the critical time—a silent, watchful presence. Six days later, when it ended, I was unable to find a proper way to thank him, and I never have, and so, if nothing else, this story represents a small gesture of gratitude twenty years overdue.

Even after two decades I can close my eyes and return to that porch at the Tip Top Lodge. I can see the old guy staring at me. Elroy Berdahl: eighty-one years old, skinny and shrunken and mostly bald. He wore a flannel shirt and brown work pants. In one hand, I remember, he carried a green apple, a small paring knife in the other. His eyes had the bluish gray color of a razor blade, the same polished shine, and as he peered up at me I felt a strange sharpness, almost painful, a cutting sensation, as if his gaze were somehow slicing me open. In part, no doubt, it was my own sense of guilt, but even so I'm absolutely certain that the old man took one look and went right to the heart of things—a kid in trouble. When I asked for a room, Elroy made a little clicking sound with his tongue. He nodded, led me out to one of the cabins, and dropped a key in my hand. I remember smiling at him. I also remember wishing I hadn't. The old man shook his head as if to tell me it wasn't worth the bother.

"Dinner at five-thirty," he said. "You eat fish?"

"Anything," I said.

Elroy grunted and said, "I'll bet."

We spent six days together at the Tip Top Lodge. Just the two of us. Tourist season was over, and there were no boats on the river, and the wilderness seemed to withdraw into a great permanent stillness. Over those six days Elroy Berdahl and I took most of our meals together. In the mornings we sometimes went out on long hikes into the woods, and at night we played Scrabble or listened to records or sat reading in front of his big stone fireplace. At times I felt the awkwardness of an intruder, but Elroy accepted me into his quiet routine without fuss or ceremony. He took my presence for granted, the same way he might've sheltered a stray cat—no wasted sighs or pity—and there was never any talk about it. Just the opposite. What I remember more than anything is the man's willful, almost ferocious silence. In all that time together, all those hours, he never asked the obvious questions: Why was I there? Why alone? Why so preoccupied? If Elroy was curious about any of this, he was careful never to put it into words.

My hunch, though, is that he already knew. At least the basics. After all, it was 1968, and guys were burning draft cards, and Canada was just a boat ride away. Elroy Berdahl was no hick. His bedroom, I remember, was cluttered with books and newspapers. He killed me at the Scrabble board, barely concentrating, and on those occasions when speech was necessary he had a way of compressing large thoughts into small, cryptic packets of language. One evening, just at sunset, he pointed up at an owl circling over the violet-lighted forest to the west. "Hey, O'Brien," he said. "There's Jesus." The man was sharp—he didn't miss much. Those razor eyes. Now and then he'd catch me staring out at the river, at the far shore, and I could almost hear the tumblers clicking in his head. Maybe I'm wrong, but I doubt it.

One thing for certain, he knew I was in desperate trouble. And he knew I couldn't talk about it. The wrong word—or even the right word—and I would've disappeared. I was wired and jittery. My skin felt too tight. After supper one evening I vomited and went back to my cabin and lay down for a few moments and then vomited again; another time, in the middle of the afternoon, I began sweating and couldn't shut it off. I went through whole days feeling dizzy with sorrow. I couldn't sleep; I couldn't lie still. At night I'd toss around in bed, half awake, half dreaming, imagining how I'd sneak down to the beach and quietly push one of the old man's boats out into the river and start paddling my way toward Canada. There were times when I thought I'd gone off the psychic edge. I couldn't tell up from down, I was just falling, and late in the night I'd lie there watching bizarre pictures spin through my head. Getting chased by the Border Patrol—helicopters and searchlights and barking dogs—I'd be crashing through the woods, I'd be down on my hands and knees—people shouting out my name—the law closing in on all sides—my hometown draft board and the FBI and the Royal Canadian Mounted Police. It all seemed crazy and impossible. Twenty-one years old, an ordinary kid with all the ordinary dreams and ambitions, and all I wanted was to live the life I was born to—a mainstream life—I loved baseball and hamburgers and cherry Cokes—and now I was off on the margins of exile, leaving my country forever, and it seemed so grotesque and terrible and sad.

I'm not sure how I made it through those six days. Most of it I can't remember. On two or three afternoons, to pass some time, I helped Elroy get the place ready for winter, sweeping down the cabins and hauling in the boats, little chores that kept my body moving. The days were cool and bright. The nights were very dark. One morning the old man showed me how to split and stack firewood, and for several hours we just worked in silence out behind his house. At one point, I remember, Elroy put down his maul and looked at me for a long time, his lips drawn as if framing a difficult question, but then he shook his head and went back to work. The man's self-control was amazing. He never pried. He never put me in a position that required lies or denials. To an extent, I suppose, his reticence was typical of that part of Minnesota, where privacy still held value, and even if I'd been walking around with some horrible deformity—four arms and three heads—I'm sure the old man would've talked about everything except those extra arms and heads. Simple politeness was part of it. But even more than that, I think, the man understood that words were insufficient. The problem had gone beyond discussion. During that long summer I'd been over and over the various arguments, all the pros and cons, and it was no longer a question that could be decided by an act of pure reason. Intellect had come up against emotion. My conscience told me to run, but some irrational and powerful force was resisting, like a weight pushing me toward the war. What it came down to, stupidly, was a sense of shame. Hot, stupid shame. I did not want people to think badly of me. Not my parents, not my brother and sister, not even the folks down at the Gobbler Café. I was ashamed to be there at the Tip Top Lodge. I was ashamed of my conscience, ashamed to be doing the right thing.

Some of this Elroy must've understood. Not the details, of course, but the plain fact of crisis.

Although the old man never confronted me about it, there was one occasion when he came close to forcing the whole thing out into the open. It was early evening, and we'd just finished supper, and over coffee and dessert I asked him about my bill, how much I owed so far. For a long while the old man squinted down at the tablecloth.

"Well, the basic rate," he said, "is fifty bucks a night. Not counting meals. This makes four nights, right?"

I nodded. I had three hundred and twelve dollars in my wallet.

Elroy kept his eyes on the tablecloth. "Now that's an on-season price. To be fair, I suppose we should knock it down a peg or two." He leaned back in his chair. "What's a reasonable number, you figure?"

"I don't know," I said. "Forty?"

"Forty's good. Forty a night. Then we tack on food—say another hundred? Two hundred sixty total?"

"I guess."

He raised his eyebrows. "Too much?"

"No, that's fair. It's fine. Tomorrow, though . . . I think I'd better take off tomorrow."

Elroy shrugged and began clearing the table. For a time he fussed with the dishes, whistling to himself as if the subject had been settled. After a second he slapped his hands together.

"You know what we forgot?" he said. "We forgot wages. Those odd jobs you done. What we have to do, we have to figure out what your time's worth. Your last job—how much did you pull in an hour?"

"Not enough," I said.

"A bad one?"

"Yes. Pretty bad."

Slowly then, without intending any long sermon, I told him about my days at the pig plant. It began as a straight recitation of the facts, but before I could stop myself I was talking about the blood clots and the water gun and how the smell had soaked into my skin and how I couldn't wash it away. I went on for a long time. I told him about wild hogs squealing in my dreams, the sounds of butchery, slaughterhouse sounds, and how I'd sometimes wake up with that greasy pig-stink in my throat.

When I was finished, Elroy nodded at me.

"Well, to be honest," he said, "when you first showed up here, I wondered about all that. The aroma, I mean. Smelled like you was awful damned fond of pork chops." The old man almost smiled. He made a snuffling sound, then sat down with a pencil and a piece of paper. "So what'd this crud job pay? Ten bucks an hour? Fifteen?"

"Less."

Elroy shook his head. "Let's make it fifteen. You put in twenty-five hours here, easy. That's three hundred seventy-five bucks total wages. We subtract the two hundred sixty for food and lodging, I still owe you a hundred and fifteen."

He took four fifties out of his shirt pocket and laid them on the table.

"Call it even," he said.

"No."

"Pick it up. Get yourself a haircut."

The money lay on the table for the rest of the evening. It was still there when I went back to my cabin. In the morning, though, I found an envelope tacked to my door. Inside were the four fifties and a two-word note that said EMERGENCY FUND.

The man knew.

· · ·

Looking back after twenty years, I sometimes wonder if the events of that summer didn't happen in some other dimension, a place where your life exists before you've lived it, and where it goes afterward. None of it ever seemed real. During my time at the Tip Top Lodge I had the feeling that I'd slipped out of my own skin, hovering a few feet away while some poor yo-yo with my name and face tried to make his way toward a future he didn't understand and didn't want. Even now I can see myself as I was then. It's like watching an old home movie: I'm young and tan and fit. I've got hair—lots of it. I don't smoke or drink. I'm wearing faded blue jeans and a white polo shirt. I can see myself sitting on Elroy Berdahl's dock near dusk one evening, the sky a bright shimmering pink, and I'm finishing up a letter to my parents that tells what I'm about to do and why I'm doing it and how sorry I am that I'd never found the courage to talk to them about it. I ask them not to be angry. I try to explain some of my feelings, but there aren't enough words, and so I just say that it's a thing that has to be done. At the end of the letter I talk about the vacations we used to take up in this north country, at a place called Whitefish Lake, and how the scenery here reminds me of those good times. I tell them I'm fine. I tell them I'll write again from Winnipeg or Montreal or wherever I end up.

On my last full day, the sixth day, the old man took me out fishing on the Rainy River. The afternoon was sunny and cold. A stiff breeze came in from the north, and I remember how the little fourteen-foot boat made sharp rocking motions as we pushed off from the dock. The current was fast. All around us, there was a vastness to the world, an unpeopled rawness, just the trees and the sky and the water reaching out toward nowhere. The air had the brittle scent of October.

For ten or fifteen minutes Elroy held a course upstream, the river choppy and silver-gray, then he turned straight north and put the engine on full throttle. I felt the bow lift beneath me. I remember the wind in my ears, the sound of the old outboard Evinrude. For a time I didn't pay attention to anything, just feeling the cold spray against my face, but then it occurred to me that at some point we must've passed into Canadian waters, across that dotted line between two different worlds, and I remember a sudden tightness in my chest as I looked up and watched the far shore come at me. This wasn't a daydream. It was tangible and real. As we came in toward land, Elroy cut the engine, letting the boat fishtail lightly about twenty yards off shore. The old man didn't look at me or speak. Bending down, he opened up his tackle box and busied himself with a bobber and a piece of wire leader, humming to himself, his eyes down.

It struck me then that he must've planned it. I'll never be certain, of course, but I think he meant to bring me up against the realities, to guide me across the river and to take me to the edge and to stand a kind of vigil as I chose a life for myself.

I remember staring at the old man, then at my hands, then at Canada. The shoreline was dense with brush and timber. I could see tiny red berries on the bushes. I could see a squirrel up in one of the birch trees, a big crow looking at me from a boulder along the river. That close—twenty yards—and I could see the delicate latticework of the leaves, the texture of the soil, the browned needles beneath the pines, the configurations of geology and human history. Twenty yards. I could've done it. I could've jumped and started swimming for my life. Inside me, in my chest, I felt a terrible squeezing pressure. Even now, as I write this, I can still feel that tightness. And I want you to feel it—the wind coming off the river, the waves, the silence, the wooded frontier. You're at the bow of a boat on the Rainy River. You're twenty-one years old, you're scared, and there's a hard squeezing pressure in your chest.

What would you do?

Would you jump? Would you feel pity for yourself? Would you think about your family and your childhood and your dreams and all you're leaving behind? Would it hurt? Would it feel like dying? Would you cry, as I did?

I tried to swallow it back. I tried to smile, except I was crying.

Now, perhaps, you can understand why I've never told this story before. It's not just the embarrassment of tears. That's part of it, no doubt, but what embarrasses me much more, and always will, is the paralysis that took my heart. A moral freeze: I couldn't decide, I couldn't act, I couldn't comport myself with even a pretense of modest human dignity.

All I could do was cry. Quietly, not bawling, just the chest-chokes.

At the rear of the boat Elroy Berdahl pretended not to notice. He held a fishing rod in his hands, his head bowed to hide his eyes. He kept humming a soft, monotonous little tune. Everywhere, it seemed, in the trees and water and sky, a great worldwide sadness came pressing down on me, a crushing sorrow, sorrow like I had never known it before.

And what was so sad, I realized, was that Canada had become a pitiful fantasy. Silly and hopeless. It was no longer a possibility. Right then, with the shore so close, I understood that I would not do what I should do. I would not swim away from my hometown and my country and my life. I would not be brave. That old image of myself as a hero, as a man of conscience and courage, all that was just a threadbare pipe dream. Bobbing there on the Rainy River, looking back at the Minnesota shore, I felt a sudden swell of helplessness come over me, a drowning sensation, as if I had toppled overboard and was being swept away by the silver waves. Chunks of my own history flashed by. I saw a seven-year-old boy in a white cowboy hat and a Lone Ranger mask and a pair of bolstered six-shooters; I saw a twelve-year-old Little League shortstop pivoting to turn a double play; I saw a sixteen-year-old kid decked out for his first prom, looking spiffy in a white tux and a black bow tie, his hair cut short and flat, his shoes freshly polished. My whole life seemed to spill out into the river, swirling away from me, everything I had ever been or ever wanted to be. I couldn't get my breath; I couldn't stay afloat; I couldn't tell which way to swim. A hallucination, I suppose, but it was as real as anything I would ever feel. I saw my parents calling to me from the far shoreline. I saw my brother and sister, all the townsfolk, the mayor and the entire Chamber of Commerce and all my old teachers and girlfriends and high school buddies. Like some outlandish sporting event: everybody screaming from the sidelines, rooting me on—a loud stadium roar. Hotdogs and popcorn—stadium smells, stadium heat. A squad of cheerleaders did cartwheels along the banks of the Rainy River; they had megaphones and pompoms and smooth brown thighs. The crowd swayed left and right. A marching band played fight songs. All my aunts and uncles were there, and Abraham Lincoln, and Saint George, and a nine-year-old girl named Linda who had died of a brain tumor back in fifth grade, and several members of the United States Senate, and a blind poet scribbling notes, and LBJ, and Huck Finn, and Abbie Hoffman, and all the dead soldiers back from the grave, and the many thousands who were later to die—villagers with terrible burns, little kids without arms or legs—yes, and the Joint Chiefs of Staff were there, and a couple of popes, and a first lieutenant named Jimmy Cross, and the last surviving veteran of the American Civil War, and Jane Fonda dressed up as Barbarella, and an old man sprawled beside a pigpen, and my grandfather, and Gary Cooper, and a kind-faced woman carrying an umbrella and a copy of Plato's *Republic*, and a million ferocious citizens waving flags of all shapes and colors—people in hard hats, people in headbands—they were all whooping and chanting and urging me toward one shore or the other. I saw faces from my distant past and distant future. My wife was there. My unborn daughter waved at me, and my two sons hopped up and down, and a drill sergeant named Blyton sneered and shot up a finger and shook his head. There was a choir in bright purple robes. There was a cabbie from the Bronx. There was a slim young man I would one day kill with a hand grenade along a red clay trail outside the village of My Khe.

The little aluminum boat rocked softly beneath me. There was the wind and the sky.

I tried to will myself overboard.

I gripped the edge of the boat and leaned forward and thought, *Now.*

I did try. It just wasn't possible.

All those eyes on me—the town, the whole universe —and I couldn't risk the embarrassment. It was as if there were an audience to my life, that swirl of faces along the river, and in my head I could hear people screaming at me. Traitor! they yelled. Turncoat! Pussy! I felt myself blush. I couldn't tolerate it. I couldn't endure the mockery, or the disgrace, or the patriotic ridicule. Even in my imagination, the shore just twenty yards away, I couldn't make myself be brave. It had nothing to do with morality. Embarrassment, that's all it was.

And right then I submitted.

I would go to the war—I would kill and maybe die—because I was embarrassed not to.

That was the sad thing. And so I sat in the bow of the boat and cried.

It was loud now. Loud, hard crying.

Elroy Berdahl remained quiet. He kept fishing. He worked his line with the tips of his fingers, patiently, squinting out at his red and white bobber on the Rainy River. His eyes were flat and impassive. He didn't speak. He was simply there, like the river and the late-summer sun. And yet by his presence, his mute watchfulness, he made it real. He was the true audience. He was a witness, like God, or like the gods, who look on in absolute silence as we live our lives, as we make our choices or fail to make them.

"Ain't biting," he said.

Then after a time the old man pulled in his line and turned the boat back toward Minnesota.

I don't remember saying goodbye. That last night we had dinner together, and I went to bed early, and in the morning

Elroy fixed breakfast for me. When I told him I'd be leaving, the old man nodded as if he already knew. He looked down at the table and smiled.

At some point later in the morning it's possible that we shook hands—I just don't remember—but I do know that by the time I'd finished packing the old man had disappeared. Around noon, when I took my suitcase out to the car, I noticed that his old black pickup truck was no longer parked in front of the main lodge. I went inside and waited for a while, but I felt a bone certainty that he wouldn't be back. In a way, I thought, it was appropriate. I washed up the breakfast dishes, left his two hundred dollars on the kitchen counter, got into the car, and drove south toward home.

The day was cloudy. I passed through towns with familiar names, through the pine forests and down to the prairie, and then to Vietnam, where I was a soldier, and then home again. I survived, but it's not a happy ending. I was a coward. I went to the war.

# Enemies

One morning in late July, while we were out on patrol near LZ Gator, Lee Strunk and Dave Jensen got into a fistfight. It was about something stupid—a missing jackknife—but even so the fight was vicious. For a while it went back and forth, but Dave Jensen was much bigger and much stronger, and eventually he wrapped an arm around Strunk's neck and pinned him down and kept hitting him on the nose. He hit him hard. And he didn't stop. Strunk's nose made a sharp snapping sound, like a firecracker, but even then Jensen kept hitting him, over and over, quick stiff punches that did not miss. It took three of us to pull him off. When it was over, Strunk had to be choppered back to the rear, where he had his nose looked after, and two days later he rejoined us wearing a metal splint and lots of gauze.

In any other circumstance it might've ended there. But this was Vietnam, where guys carried guns, and Dave Jensen started to worry. It was mostly in his head. There were no threats, no vows of revenge, just a silent tension between them that made Jensen take special precautions. On patrol he was careful to keep track of Strunk's whereabouts. He dug his foxholes on the far side of the perimeter; he kept his back covered; he avoided situations that might put the two of them alone together. Eventually, after a week of this, the strain began to create problems. Jensen couldn't relax. Like fighting two different wars, he said. No safe ground: enemies everywhere. No front or rear. At night he had trouble sleeping—a skittish feeling—always on guard, hearing strange noises in the dark, imagining a grenade rolling into his foxhole or the tickle of a knife against his ear. The distinction between good guys and bad guys disappeared for him. Even in times of relative safety, while the rest of us took it easy, Jensen would be sitting with his back against a stone wall, weapon across his knees, watching Lee Strunk with quick, nervous eyes. It got to the point finally where he lost control. Something must've snapped. One afternoon he began firing his weapon into the air, yelling Strunk's name, just firing and yelling, and it didn't stop until he'd rattled off an entire magazine of ammunition. We were all flat on the ground. Nobody had the nerve to go near him. Jensen started to reload, but then suddenly he sat down and held his head in his arms and wouldn't move. For two or three hours he simply sat there.

But that wasn't the bizarre part.

Because late that same night he borrowed a pistol, gripped it by the barrel, and used it like a hammer to break his own nose.

Afterward, he crossed the perimeter to Lee Strunk's foxhole. He showed him what he'd done and asked if every-thing was square between them.

Strunk nodded and said, Sure, things were square.

But in the morning Lee Strunk couldn't stop laughing. "The man's crazy," he said. "I stole his fucking jackknife."

# Friends

Dave Jensen and Lee Strunk did not become instant buddies, but they did learn to trust each other. Over the next month they often teamed up on ambushes. They covered each other on patrol, shared a foxhole, took turns pulling guard at night. In late August they made a pact that if one of them should ever get totally fucked up—a wheelchair wound—the other guy would automatically find a way to end it. As far as I could tell they were serious. They drew it up on paper, signing their names and asking a couple of guys to act as witnesses. And then in October Lee Strunk stepped on a rigged mortar round. It took off his right leg at the knee. He managed a funny little half step, like a hop, then he tilted sideways and dropped. "Oh, damn," he said. For a while he kept on saying it, "Damn oh damn," as if he'd stubbed a toe. Then he panicked. He tried to get up and run, but there was nothing left to run on. He fell hard. The stump of his right leg was twitching. There were slivers of bone, and the blood came in quick spurts like water from a pump. He seemed bewildered. He reached down as if to massage his missing leg, then he passed out, and Rat Kiley put on a tourniquet and administered morphine and ran plasma into him.

There was nothing much anybody could do except wait for the dustoff. After we'd secured an LZ, Dave Jensen went over and kneeled at Strunk's side. The stump had stopped twitching now. For a time there was some question as to whether Strunk was still alive, but then he opened his eyes and looked up at Dave Jensen. "Oh, Jesus," he said, and moaned, and tried to slide away and said, "Jesus, man, don't kill me."

"Relax," Jensen said.

Lee Strunk seemed groggy and confused. He lay still for a second and then motioned toward his leg. "Really, it's not so bad. Not terrible. Hey, *really*—they can sew it back on—*really.*"

"Right, I'll bet they can."

"You think?"

"Sure I do."

Strunk frowned at the sky. He passed out again, then woke up and said, "Don't kill me."

"I won't," Jensen said.

"I'm *serious.*"

"Sure."

"But you got to promise. Swear it to me—swear you won't kill me."

Jensen nodded and said, "I swear," and then a little later we carried Strunk to the dustoff chopper. Jensen reached out and touched the good leg. "Go on now," he said. Later we heard that Strunk died somewhere over Chu Lai, which seemed to relieve Dave Jensen of an enormous weight.

# How to Tell a True War Story

This is true. I had a buddy in Vietnam. His name was Bob Kiley, but everybody called him Rat.

A friend of his gets killed, so about a week later Rat sits down and writes a letter to the guy's sister. Rat tells her what a great brother she had, how together the guy was, a number one pal and comrade. A real soldier's soldier, Rat says. Then he tells a few stories to make the point, how her brother would always volunteer for stuff nobody else would volunteer for in a million years, dangerous stuff, like doing recon or going out on these really badass night patrols. Stainless steel balls, Rat tells her. The guy was a little crazy, for sure, but crazy in a good way, a real daredevil, because he liked the challenge of it, he liked testing himself, just man against gook. A great, great guy, Rat says.

Anyway, it's a terrific letter, very personal and touching. Rat almost bawls writing it. He gets all teary telling about the good times they had together, how her brother made the war seem almost fun, always raising hell and lighting up villes and bringing smoke to bear every which way. A great sense of humor, too. Like the time at this river when he went fishing with a whole damn crate of hand grenades. Probably the funniest thing in world history, Rat says, all that gore, about twenty zillion dead gook fish. Her brother, he had the right attitude. He knew how to have a good time. On Halloween, this real hot spooky night, the dude paints up his body all different colors and puts on this weird mask and hikes over to a ville and goes trick-or-treating almost stark naked, just boots and balls and an M-16. A tremendous human being, Rat says. Pretty nutso sometimes, but you could trust him with your life.

And then the letter gets very sad and serious. Rat pours his heart out. He says he loved the guy. He says the guy was his best friend in the world. They were like soul mates, he says, like twins or something, they had a whole lot in common. He tells the guy's sister he'll look her up when the war's over.

So what happens?

Rat mails the letter. He waits two months. The dumb cooze never writes back.

A true war story is never moral. It does not instruct, nor encourage virtue, nor suggest models of proper human behavior, nor restrain men from doing the things men have always done. If a story seems moral, do not believe it. If at the end of a war story you feel uplifted, or if you feel that some small bit of rectitude has been salvaged from the larger waste, then you have been made the victim of a very old and terrible lie. There is no rectitude whatsoever. There is no virtue. As a first rule of thumb, therefore, you can tell a true war story by its absolute and uncompromising allegiance to obscenity and evil. Listen to Rat Kiley. Cooze, he says. He does not say bitch. He certainly does not say woman, or girl. He says cooze. Then he spits and stares. He's nineteen years old—it's too much for him—so he looks at you with those big sad gentle killer eyes and says cooze, because his friend is dead, and because it's so incredibly sad and true: she never wrote back.

You can tell a true war story if it embarrasses you. If you don't care for obscenity, you don't care for the truth; if you don't care for the truth, watch how you vote. Send guys to war, they come home talking dirty.

Listen to Rat: "Jesus Christ, man, I write this beautiful fuckin' letter, I slave over it, and what happens? The dumb cooze never writes back."

The dead guy's name was Curt Lemon. What happened was, we crossed a muddy river and marched west into the mountains, and on the third day we took a break along a trail junction in deep jungle. Right away, Lemon and Rat Kiley started goofing. They didn't understand about the spookiness. They were kids; they just didn't know. A nature hike, they thought, not even a war, so they went off into the shade of some giant trees—quadruple canopy, no sunlight at all—and they were giggling and calling each other yellow mother and playing a silly game they'd invented. The game involved smoke grenades, which were harmless unless you did stupid things, and what they did was pull out the pin and stand a few feet apart and play catch under the shade of those huge trees. Whoever chickened out was a yellow mother. And if nobody chickened out, the grenade would make a light popping sound and they'd be covered with smoke and they'd laugh and dance around and then do it again.

It's all exactly true.

It happened, to *me*, nearly twenty years ago, and I still remember that trail junction and those giant trees and a soft dripping sound somewhere beyond the trees. I remember the smell of moss. Up in the canopy there were tiny white blossoms, but no sunlight at all, and I remember the shadows spreading out under the trees where Curt Lemon and Rat Kiley were playing catch with smoke grenades. Mitchell Sanders sat flipping his yo-yo. Norman Bowker and Kiowa and Dave Jensen were dozing, or half dozing, and all around us were those ragged green mountains.

Except for the laughter things were quiet.

At one point, I remember, Mitchell Sanders turned and looked at me, not quite nodding, as if to warn me about something, and then after a while he rolled up his yo-yo and moved away.

It's hard to tell you what happened next.

They were just goofing. There was a noise, I suppose, which must've been the detonator, so I glanced behind me and watched Lemon step from the shade into bright sunlight. His face was suddenly brown and shining. A handsome kid, really. Sharp gray eyes, lean and narrow-waisted, and when he died it was almost beautiful, the way the sunlight came around him and lifted him up and sucked him high into a tree full of moss and vines and white blossoms.

In any war story, but especially a true one, it's difficult to separate what happened from what seemed to happen. What seems to happen becomes its own happening and has to be told that way. The angles of vision are skewed. When a booby trap explodes, you close your eyes and duck and float outside yourself. When a guy dies, like Curt Lemon, you look away and then look back for a moment and then look away again. The pictures get jumbled; you tend to miss a lot. And then afterward, when you go to tell about it, there is always that surreal seemingness, which makes the story seem untrue, but which in fact represents the hard and exact truth as it *seemed*.

In many cases a true war story cannot be believed. If you believe it, be skeptical. It's a question of credibility. Often the crazy stuff is true and the normal stuff isn't, because the normal stuff is necessary to make you believe the truly incredible craziness.

In other cases you can't even tell a true war story. Sometimes it's just beyond telling.

I heard this one, for example, from Mitchell Sanders. It was near dusk and we were sitting at my foxhole along a wide muddy river north of Quang Ngai City. I remember how peaceful the twilight was. A deep pinkish red spilled out on the river, which moved without sound, and in the morning we would cross the river and march west into the mountains. The occasion was right for a good story.

"God's truth," Mitchell Sanders said. "A six-man patrol goes up into the mountains on a basic listening-post operation. The idea's to spend a week up there, just lie low and listen for enemy movement. They've got a radio along, so if they hear anything suspicious — anything — they're supposed to call in artillery or gunships, whatever it takes. Otherwise they keep strict field discipline. Absolute silence. They just listen."

Sanders glanced at me to make sure I had the scenario. He was playing with his yo-yo, dancing it with short, tight strokes of the wrist.

His face was blank in the dusk.

"We're talking regulation, by-the-book LP. These six guys, they don't say boo for a solid week. They don't got tongues. *All* ears."

"Right," I said.

"Understand me?"

"Invisible."

Sanders nodded.

"Affirm," he said. "Invisible. So what happens is, these guys get themselves deep in the bush, all camouflaged up, and they lie down and wait and that's all they do, nothing else, they lie there for seven straight days and just listen. And man, I'll tell you—it's spooky. This is mountains. You don't *know* spooky till you been there. Jungle, sort of, except it's way up in the clouds and there's always this fog—like rain, except it's not raining—everything's all wet and swirly and tangled up and you can't see jack, you can't find your own pecker to piss with. Like you don't even have a body. Serious spooky. You just go with the vapors—the fog sort of takes you in . . . And the sounds, man. The sounds carry forever. You hear stuff nobody should ever hear.

Sanders was quiet for a second, just working the yo-yo, then he smiled at me.

"So after a couple days the guys start hearing this real soft, kind of wacked-out music. Weird echoes and stuff. Like a radio or something, but it's not a radio, it's this strange gook music that comes right out of the rocks. Faraway, sort of, but right up close, too. They try to ignore it. But it's a listening post, right? So they listen. And every night they keep hearing that crazyass gook concert. All kinds of chimes and xylophones. I mean, this is wilderness—no way, it can't be real—but there it is, like the mountains are tuned in to Radio fucking Hanoi. Naturally they get nervous. One guy sticks Juicy Fruit in his ears. Another guy almost flips. Thing is, though, they can't report music. They can't get on the horn and call back to base and say, 'Hey, listen, we need some firepower, we got to blow away this weirdo gook rock band.' They can't do that. It wouldn't go down. So they lie there in the fog and keep their mouths shut. And what makes it extra bad, see, is the poor dudes can't horse around like normal. Can't joke it away. Can't even talk to each other except maybe in whispers, all hush-hush, and that just revs up the willies. All they do is listen."

Again there was some silence as Mitchell Sanders looked out on the river. The dark was coming on hard now, and off to the west I could see the mountains rising in silhouette, all the mysteries and unknowns.

"This next part," Sanders said quietly, "you won't believe."

"Probably not," I said.

"You won't. And you know why?" He gave me a long, tired smile. "Because it happened. Because every word is absolutely dead-on true."

Sanders made a sound in his throat, like a sigh, as if to say he didn't care if I believed him or not. But he did care. He wanted me to feel the truth, to believe by the raw force of feeling. He seemed sad, in a way.

"These six guys," he said, "they're pretty fried out by now, and one night they start hearing voices. Like at a cocktail party. That's what it sounds like, this big swank gook cocktail party somewhere out there in the fog. Music and chitchat and stuff. It's crazy, I know, but they hear the champagne corks. They hear the actual martini glasses. Real hoity-toity, all very civilized, except this isn't civilization. This is Nam.

"Anyway, the guys try to be cool. They just lie there and groove, but after a while they start hearing—you won't believe this—they hear chamber music. They hear violins and cellos. They hear this terrific mama-san soprano. Then after a while they hear gook opera and a glee club and the Haiphong Boys Choir and a barbershop quartet and all kinds of funky chanting and Buddha-Buddha stuff. And the whole time, in the background, there's still that cocktail party going on. All these different voices. Not human voices, though. Because it's the mountains. Follow me? The rock—it's *talking*. And the fog, too, and the grass and the goddamn mongooses. Everything talks. The trees talk politics, the monkeys talk religion. The whole country. Vietnam. The place talks. It talks. Understand? Nam—it truly *talks*.

"The guys can't cope. They lose it. They get on the radio and report enemy movement—a whole army, they say—and they order up the firepower. They get arty and gunships. They call in air strikes. And I'll tell you, they fuckin' crash that cocktail party. All night long, they just smoke those mountains. They make jungle juice. They blow away trees and glee clubs and whatever else there is to blow away. Scorch time. They walk napalm up and down the ridges. They bring in the Cobras and F-4s, they use Willie Peter and HE and incendiaries. It's all fire. They make those mountains burn.

"Around dawn things finally get quiet. Like you never even *heard* quiet before. One of those real thick, real misty days—just clouds and fog, they're off in this special zone —and the mountains are absolutely dead-flat silent. Like *Brigadoon*—pure vapor, you know? Everything's all sucked up inside the fog. Not a single sound, except they still *hear* it.

"So they pack up and start humping. They head down the mountain, back to base camp, and when they get there they don't say diddly. They don't talk. Not a word, like they're deaf and dumb. Later on this fat bird colonel comes up and asks what the hell happened out there. What'd they hear? Why all the ordnance? The man's ragged out, he gets down tight on their case. I mean, they spent six trillion dollars on firepower, and this fatass colonel wants answers, he wants to know what the fuckin' story is.

"But the guys don't say zip. They just look at him for a while, sort of funny like, sort of amazed, and the whole war is right there in that stare. It says everything you can't ever say. It says, man, you got *wax* in your ears. It says, poor bastard, you'll never know—wrong frequency—you don't *even* want to hear this. Then they salute the fucker and walk away, because certain stories you don't ever tell."

You can tell a true war story by the way it never seems to end. Not then, not ever. Not when Mitchell Sanders stood up and moved off into the dark.

It all happened.

Even now, at this instant, I remember that yo-yo. In a way, I suppose, you had to be there, you had to hear it, but I could tell how desperately Sanders wanted me to believe him, his frustration at not quite getting the details right, not quite pinning down the final and definitive truth.

And I remember sitting at my foxhole that night, watching the shadows of Quang Ngai, thinking about the coming day and how we would cross the river and march west into the mountains, all the ways I might die, all the things I did not understand.

Late in the night Mitchell Sanders touched my shoulder. "Just came to me," he whispered. "The moral, I mean. Nobody listens. Nobody hears nothin'. Like that fatass colonel. The politicians, all the civilian types. Your girlfriend. My girlfriend. Everybody's sweet little virgin girlfriend. What they need is to go out on LP. The vapors, man. Trees and rocks—you got to *listen* to your enemy."

And then again, in the morning, Sanders came up to me. The platoon was preparing to move out, checking weapons, going through all the rituals that preceded a day's march. Already the lead squad had crossed the river and was filing off toward the west.

"I got a confession to make," Sanders said. "Last night, man, I had to make up a few things."

"I know that."

"The glee club. There wasn't any glee club."

"Right."

"No opera."

"Forget it, I understand."

"Yeah, but listen, it's still true. Those six guys, they heard wicked sound out there. They heard sound you just plain won't believe. "

Sanders pulled on his rucksack, closed his eyes for a moment, and let out a short, throat-clearing sigh. I knew what was coming.

"All right," I said, "what's the moral?"

"Forget it."

"No, go ahead."

For a long while he was quiet, looking away, and the silence kept stretching out until it was almost embarrassing. Then he shrugged and gave me a stare that lasted all day.

"Hear that quiet, man?" he said. "That quiet—just listen. There's your moral."

In a true war story, if there's a moral at all, it's like the thread that makes the cloth. You can't tease it out. You can't extract the meaning without unraveling the deeper meaning. And in the end, really, there's nothing much to say about a true war story, except maybe "Oh."

True war stories do not generalize. They do not indulge in abstraction or analysis.

For example: War is hell. As a moral declaration the old truism seems perfectly true, and yet because it abstracts, because it generalizes, I can't believe it with my stomach. Nothing turns inside.

It comes down to gut instinct. A true war story, if truly told, makes the stomach believe.

This one does it for me. I've told it before—many times, many versions—but here's what actually happened.

We crossed that river and marched west into the mountains. On the third day, Curt Lemon stepped on a booby-trapped 105 round. He was playing catch with Rat Kiley, laughing, and then he was dead. The trees were thick; it took nearly an hour to cut an LZ for the dustoff.

Later, higher in the mountains, we came across a baby VC

water buffalo. What it was doing there I don't know—no farms or paddies—but we chased it down and got a rope around it and led it along to a deserted village where we set up for the night. After supper Rat Kiley went over and stroked its nose.

He opened up a can of C rations, pork and beans, but the baby buffalo wasn't interested.

Rat shrugged.

He stepped back and shot it through the right front knee. The animal did not make a sound. It went down hard, then got up again, and Rat took careful aim and shot off an ear. He shot it in the hindquarters and in the little hump at its back. He shot it twice in the flanks. It wasn't to kill; it was to hurt. He put the rifle muzzle up against the mouth and shot the mouth away. Nobody said much. The whole platoon stood there watching, feeling all kinds of things, but there wasn't a great deal of pity for the baby water buffalo. Curt Lemon was dead. Rat Kiley had lost his best friend in the world. Later in the week he would write a long personal letter to the guy's sister, who would not write back, but for now it was a question of pain. He shot off the tail. He shot away chunks of meat below the ribs. All around us there was the smell of smoke and filth and deep greenery, and the evening was humid and very hot. Rat went to automatic. He shot randomly, almost casually, quick little spurts in the belly and butt. Then he reloaded, squatted down, and shot it in the left front knee. Again the animal fell hard and tried to get up, but this time it couldn't quite make it. It wobbled and went down sideways. Rat shot it in the nose. He bent forward and whispered something, as if talking to a pet, then he shot it in the throat. All the while the baby buffalo was silent, or almost silent, just a light bubbling sound where the nose had been. It lay very still. Nothing moved except the eyes, which were enormous, the pupils shiny black and dumb.

Rat Kiley was crying. He tried to say something, but then cradled his rifle and went off by himself.

The rest of us stood in a ragged circle around the baby buffalo. For a time no one spoke. We had witnessed something essential, something brand-new and profound, a piece of the world so startling there was not yet a name for it.

Somebody kicked the baby buffalo.

It was still alive, though just barely, just in the eyes.

"Amazing," Dave Jensen said. "My whole life, I never seen anything like it."

"Never?"

"Not hardly. Not once."

Kiowa and Mitchell Sanders picked up the baby buffalo. They hauled it across the open square, hoisted it up, and dumped it in the village well.

Afterward, we sat waiting for Rat to get himself together.

"Amazing," Dave Jensen kept saying. "A new wrinkle. I never seen it before."

Mitchell Sanders took out his yo-yo. "Well, that's Nam," he said. "Garden of Evil. Over here, man, every sin's real fresh and original."

How do you generalize?

War is hell, but that's not the half of it, because war is also mystery and terror and adventure and courage and discovery and holiness and pity and despair and longing and love. War is nasty; war is fun. War is thrilling; war is drudgery. War makes you a man; war makes you dead.

The truths are contradictory. It can be argued, for instance, that war is grotesque. But in truth war is also beauty. For all its horror, you can't help but gape at the awful majesty of combat. You stare out at tracer rounds unwinding through the dark like brilliant red ribbons. You crouch in ambush as a cool, impassive moon rises over the night-time paddies. You admire the fluid symmetries of troops on the move, the harmonies of sound and shape and proportion, the great sheets of metal-fire streaming down from a gunship, the illumination rounds, the white phosphorus, the purply orange glow of napalm, the rocket's red glare. It's not pretty, exactly. It's astonishing. It fills the eye. It commands you. You hate it, yes, but your eyes do not. Like a killer forest fire, like cancer under a microscope, any battle or bombing raid or artillery barrage has the aesthetic purity of absolute moral indifference—a powerful, implacable beauty—and a true war story will tell the truth about this, though the truth is ugly.

To generalize about war is like generalizing about peace. Almost everything is true. Almost nothing is true. At its core, perhaps, war is just another name for death, and yet any soldier will tell you, if he tells the truth, that proximity to death brings with it a corresponding proximity to life. After a fire-fight, there is always the immense pleasure of aliveness. The trees are alive. The grass, the soil—everything. All around you things are purely living, and you among them, and the aliveness makes you tremble. You feel an intense, out-of-the-skin awareness of your living self—your truest self, the human being you want to be and then become by the force of wanting it. In the midst of evil you want to be a good man. You want decency. You want justice and courtesy and human concord, things you never knew you wanted. There is a kind of largeness to it, a kind of godliness. Though it's odd, you're never more alive than when you're almost dead. You recognize what's valuable. Freshly, as if for the first time, you love what's best in yourself and in the world, all that might be lost. At the hour of dusk you sit at your foxhole and look out on a wide river turning pinkish red, and at the mountains beyond, and although in the morning you must cross the river and go into the mountains and do terrible things and maybe die, even so, you find yourself studying the fine colors on the river, you feel wonder and awe at the setting of the sun, and you are filled with a hard, aching love for how the world could be and always should be, but now is not.

Mitchell Sanders was right. For the common soldier, at least, war has the feel—the spiritual texture—of a great ghostly fog, thick and permanent. There is no clarity. Everything swirls. The old rules are no longer binding, the old truths no longer true. Right spills over into wrong. Order blends into chaos, love into hate, ugliness into beauty, law into anarchy, civility into savagery. The vapors suck you in. You can't tell where you are, or why you're there, and the only certainty is overwhelming ambiguity.

In war you lose your sense of the definite, hence your sense of truth itself, and therefore it's safe to say that in a true war story nothing is ever absolutely true.

Often in a true war story there is not even a point, or else the point doesn't hit you until twenty years later, in your sleep, and you wake up and shake your wife and start telling the story to her, except when you get to the end you've forgotten the point again. And then for a long time you lie there watching the story happen in your head. You listen to your wife's breathing. The war's over. You close your eyes. You take a feeble swipe at the dark and think, Christ, what's the *point?*

This one wakes me up.

In the mountains that day, I watched Lemon turn sideways. He laughed and said something to Rat Kiley. Then he took a peculiar half step, moving from shade into bright sunlight, and the booby-trapped 105 round blew him into a tree. The parts were just hanging there, so Dave Jensen and I were ordered to shinny up and peel him off. I remember the white bone of an arm. I remember pieces of skin and something wet and yellow that must've been the intestines. The gore was horrible, and stays with me. But what wakes me up twenty years later is Dave Jensen singing "Lemon Tree" as we threw down the parts.

You can tell a true war story by the questions you ask. Somebody tells a story, let's say, and afterward you ask, "Is it true?" and if the answer matters, you've got your answer.

For example, we've all heard this one. Four guys go down a trail. A grenade sails out. One guy jumps on it and takes the blast and saves his three buddies.

Is it true?

The answer matters.

You'd feel cheated if it never happened. Without the grounding reality, it's just a trite bit of puffery, pure Hollywood, untrue in the way all such stories are untrue. Yet even if it did happen—and maybe it did, anything's possible —even then you know it can't be true, because a true war story does not depend upon that kind of truth. Absolute occurrence is irrelevant. A thing may happen and be a total lie; another thing may not happen and be truer than the truth. For example: Four guys go down a trail. A grenade sails out. One guy jumps on it and takes the blast, but it's a killer grenade and everybody dies anyway. Before they die, though, one of the dead guys says, "The fuck you do *that* for?" and the jumper says, "Story of my life, man," and the other guy starts to smile but he's dead. That's a true story that never happened.

Twenty years later, I can still see the sunlight on Lemon's face. I can see him turning, looking back at Rat Kiley, then he laughed and took that curious half step from shade into sunlight, his face suddenly brown and shining, and when his foot touched down, in that instant, he must've thought it was the sunlight that was killing him. It was not the sunlight. It was a rigged 105 round. But if I could ever get the story right, how the sun seemed to gather around him and pick him up and lift him high into a tree, if I could somehow recreate the fatal whiteness of that light, the quick glare, the obvious cause and effect, then you would believe the last thing Curt Lemon believed, which for him must've been the final truth.

Now and then, when I tell this story, someone will come up to me afterward and say she liked it. It's always a woman. Usually it's an older woman of kindly temperament and humane politics. She'll explain that as a rule she hates war stories; she can't understand why people want to wallow in all the blood and gore. But this one she liked. The poor baby buffalo, it made her sad. Sometimes, even, there are little tears. What I should do, she'll say, is put it all behind me. Find new stories to tell.

I won't say it but I'll think it.

I'll picture Rat Kiley's face, his grief, and I'll think, *You dumb cooze*.

Because she wasn't listening.

It *wasn't* a war story. It was a *love* story.

But you can't say that. All you can do is tell it one more time, patiently, adding and subtracting, making up a few things to get at the real truth. No Mitchell Sanders, you tell her. No Lemon, no Rat Kiley. No trail junction. No baby buffalo. No vines or moss or white blossoms. Beginning to end, you tell her, it's all made up. Every goddamn detail—the mountains and the river and especially that poor dumb baby buffalo. None of it happened. None of it. And even if it did happen, it didn't happen in the mountains, it happened in this little village on the Batangan Peninsula, and it was raining like crazy, and one night a guy named Stink Harris woke up screaming with a leech on his tongue. You can tell a true war story if you just keep on telling it.

And in the end, of course, a true war story is never about war. It's about sunlight. It's about the special way that dawn spreads out on a river when you know you must cross the river and march into the mountains and do things you are afraid to do. It's about love and memory. It's about sorrow. It's about sisters who never write back and people who never listen.

# The Dentist

When Curt Lemon was killed, I found it hard to mourn. I knew him only slightly, and what I did know was not impressive. He had a tendency to play the tough soldier role, always posturing, always puffing himself up, and on occasion he took it way too far. It's true that he pulled off some dangerous stunts, even a few that seemed plain crazy, like the time he painted up his body and put on a ghost mask and went out trick-or-treating on Halloween. But afterward he couldn't stop bragging. He kept replaying his own exploits, tacking on little flourishes that never happened. He had an opinion of himself, I think, that was too high for his own good. Or maybe it was the reverse. Maybe it was a low opinion that he kept trying to erase.

In any case, it's easy to get sentimental about the dead, and to guard against that I want to tell a quick Curt Lemon story.

In February we were working an area of operations called the Rocket Pocket, which got its name from the fact that the enemy sometimes used the place to launch rocket attacks on the airfield at Chu Lai. But for us it was like a two-week vacation. The AO lay along the South China Sea, where things had the feel of a resort, with white beaches and palm trees and friendly little villages. It was a quiet time. No casualties, no contact at all. As usual, though, the higher-ups couldn't leave well enough alone, and one afternoon an Army dentist was choppered in to check our teeth and do minor repair work. He was a tall, skinny young captain with bad breath. For a half hour he lectured us on oral hygiene, demonstrating the proper flossing and brushing techniques, then afterward he opened up shop in a small field tent and we all took turns going in for personal exams. At best it was a very primitive setup. There was a battery-powered drill, a canvas cot, a bucket of sea water for rinsing, a metal suitcase full of the various instruments. It amounted to assembly-line dentistry, quick and impersonal, and the young captain's main concern seemed to be the clock.

As we sat waiting, Curt Lemon began to tense up. He kept fidgeting, playing with his dog tags. Finally somebody asked what the problem was, and Lemon looked down at his hands and said that back in high school he'd had a couple of bad experiences with dentists. Real sadism, he said. Torture chamber stuff. He didn't mind blood or pain—he actually enjoyed combat—but there was something about a dentist that just gave him the creeps. He glanced over at the field tent and said, "No way. Count me out. Nobody messes with *these* teeth."

But a few minutes later, when the dentist called his name, Lemon stood up and walked into the tent.

It was over fast. He fainted even before the man touched him.

Four of us had to hoist him up and lay him on the cot.

When he came to, there was a funny new look on his face, almost sheepish, as if he'd been caught committing some terrible crime. He wouldn't talk to anyone. For the rest of the day he stayed off by himself, sitting alone under a tree, just staring down at the field tent. He seemed a little dazed. Now and then we could hear him cussing, bawling himself out. Anyone else would've laughed it off, but for Curt Lemon it was too much. The embarrassment must've turned a screw in his head. Late that night he crept down to the dental tent. He switched on a flashlight, woke up the young captain, and told him he had a monster toothache. A killer, he said—like a nail in his jaw. The dentist couldn't find any problem, but Lemon kept insisting, so the man finally shrugged and shot in the Novocain and yanked out a perfectly good tooth. There was some pain, no doubt, but in the morning Curt Lemon was all smiles.

# Sweetheart of the Song Tra Bong

Vietnam was full of strange stories, some improbable, some well beyond that, but the stories that will last forever are those that swirl back and forth across the border between trivia and bedlam, the mad and the mundane. This one keeps returning to me. I heard it from Rat Kiley, who swore up and down to its truth, although in the end, I'll admit, that doesn't amount to much of a warranty. Among the men in Alpha Company, Rat had a reputation for exaggeration and overstatement, a compulsion to rev up the facts, and for most of us it was normal procedure to discount sixty or seventy percent of anything he had to say. If Rat told you, for example, that he'd slept with four girls one night, you could figure it was about a girl and a half. It wasn't a question of deceit. Just the opposite: he wanted to heat up the truth, to make it burn so hot that you would feel exactly what he felt. For Rat Kiley, I think, facts were formed by sensation, not the other way around, and when you listened to one of his stories, you'd find yourself performing rapid calculations in your head, subtracting superlatives, figuring the square root of an absolute and then multiplying by maybe.

Still, with this particular story, Rat never backed down. He claimed to have witnessed the incident with his own eyes, and I remember how upset he became one morning when Mitchell Sanders challenged him on its basic premise.

"It can't happen," Sanders said. "Nobody ships his honey over to Nam. It don't ring true. I mean, you just can't import your own personal poontang."

Rat shook his head. "I *saw* it, man. I was right there. This guy did it."

"His girlfriend?"

"Straight on. It's a fact." Rat's voice squeaked a little. He paused and looked at his hands. "Listen, the guy sends her the money. Flies her over. This cute blonde—just a kid, just barely out of high school—she shows up with a suitcase and one of those plastic cosmetic bags. Comes right out to the boonies. I swear to God, man, she's got on culottes. White culottes and this sexy pink sweater. There she *is*."

I remember Mitchell Sanders folding his arms. He looked over at me for a second, not quite grinning, not saying a word, but I could read the amusement in his eyes.

Rat saw it, too.

"No lie," he muttered. "Culottes."

When he first arrived in-country, before joining Alpha Company, Rat had been assigned to a small medical detachment up in the mountains west of Chu Lai, near the village of Tra Bong, where along with eight other enlisted men he ran an aid station that provided basic emergency and trauma care. Casualties were flown in by helicopter, stabilized, then shipped out to hospitals in Chu Lai or Danang. It was gory work, Rat said, but predictable. Amputations, mostly—legs and feet. The area was heavily mined, thick with Bouncing Betties and homemade booby traps. For a medic, though, it was ideal duty, and Rat counted himself lucky. There was plenty of cold beer, three hot meals a day, a tin roof over his head. No humping at all. No officers, either. You could let your hair grow, he said, and you didn't have to polish your boots or snap off salutes or put up with the usual rear-eche-lon nonsense. The highest ranking NCO was an E-6 named Eddie Diamond, whose pleasures ran from dope to Darvon, and except for a rare field inspection there was no such thing as military discipline.

As Rat described it, the compound was situated at the top of a flat-crested hill along the northern outskirts of Tra Bong. At one end was a small dirt helipad; at the other end, in a rough semicircle, the mess hall and medical hootches overlooked a river called the Song Tra Bong. Surrounding the place were tangled rolls of concertina wire, with bun-kers and reinforced firing positions at staggered intervals, and base security was provided by a mixed unit of RFs, PFs, and ARVN infantry. Which is to say virtually no security at all. As soldiers, the ARVNs were useless; the Ruff-and-Puffs were outright dangerous. And yet even with decent troops the place was clearly indefensible. To the north and west the country rose up in thick walls of wilderness, triple-canopied jungle, mountains unfolding into higher mountains, ravines and gorges and fast-moving rivers and waterfalls and exotic butterflies and steep cliffs and smoky little hamlets and great valleys of bamboo and elephant grass. Originally, in the early 1960s, the place had been set up as a Special Forces outpost, and when Rat Kiley arrived nearly a decade later, a squad of six Green Berets still used the compound as a base of operations. The Greenies were not social animals. Animals, Rat said, but far from social. They had their own hootch at the edge of the perimeter, fortified with sandbags and a metal fence, and except for the bare essentials they avoided contact with the medical detachment. Secretive and suspicious, loners by nature, the six Greenies would sometimes vanish for days at a time, or even weeks, then late in the night they would just as magically reappear, moving like shadows through the moonlight, filing in silently from the dense rain forest off to the west. Among the medics there were jokes about this, but no one asked questions.

While the outpost was isolated and vulnerable, Rat said, he always felt a curious sense of safety there. Nothing much ever happened. The place was never mortared, never taken under fire, and the war seemed to be somewhere far away. On occasion, when casualties came in, there were quick spurts of activity, but otherwise the days flowed by without incident, a smooth and peaceful time. Most mornings were spent on the volleyball court. In the heat of midday the men would head for the shade, lazing away the long afternoons, and after sundown there were movies and card games and sometimes all-night drinking sessions.

It was during one of those late nights that Eddie Diamond first brought up the tantalizing possibility. It was an offhand comment. A joke, really. What they should do, Eddie said, was pool some bucks and bring in a few mama-sans from Saigon, spice things up, and after a moment one of the men laughed and said, "Our own little EM club," and somebody else said, "Hey, yeah, we pay our fuckin' dues, don't we?" It was nothing serious. Just passing time, playing with the possibilities, and so for a while they tossed the idea around, how you could actually get away with it, no officers or anything, nobody to clamp down, then they dropped the subject and moved on to cars and baseball.

Later in the night, though, a young medic named Mark Fossie kept coming back to the subject.

"Look, if you think about it," he said, "it's not that crazy. You could actually do it."

"Do what?" Rat said.

"You know. Bring in a girl. I mean, what's the problem?"

Rat shrugged. "Nothing. A war."

"Well, see, that's the thing," Mark Fossie said. "No war *here*. You could really do it. A pair of solid brass balls, that's all you'd need."

There was some laughter, and Eddie Diamond told him he'd best strap down his dick, but Fossie just frowned and looked at the ceiling for a while and then went off to write a letter.

Six weeks later his girlfriend showed up.

The way Rat told it, she came in by helicopter along with the daily resupply shipment out of Chu Lai. A tall, big-boned blonde. At best, Rat said, she was seventeen years old, fresh out of Cleveland Heights Senior High. She had long white legs and blue eyes and a complexion like strawberry ice cream. Very friendly, too.

At the helipad that morning, Mark Fossie grinned and put his arm around her and said, "Guys, this is Mary Anne."

The girl seemed tired and somewhat lost, but she smiled.

There was a heavy silence. Eddie Diamond, the ranking NCO, made a small motion with his hand, and some of the others murmured a word or two, then they watched Mark Fossie pick up her suitcase and lead her by the arm down to the hootches. For a long while the men were quiet.

"That fucker," somebody finally said.

At evening chow Mark Fossie explained how he'd set it up. Expensive, he admitted, and the logistics were complicated, but it wasn't like going to the moon. Cleveland to Los Angeles, LA to Bangkok, Bangkok to Saigon. She'd hopped a C-130 up to Chu Lai and stayed overnight at the USO and the next morning hooked a ride west with the resupply chopper.

"A cinch," Fossie said, and gazed down at his pretty girlfriend. "Thing is, you just got to *want* it enough."

Mary Anne Bell and Mark Fossie had been sweethearts since grammar school. From the sixth grade on they had known for a fact that someday they would be married, and live in a fine gingerbread house near Lake Erie, and have three healthy yellow-haired children, and grow old together, and no doubt die in each other's arms and be buried in the same walnut casket. That was the plan. They were very much in love, full of dreams, and in the ordinary flow of their lives the whole scenario might well have come true.

On that first night they set up house in one of the bunkers along the perimeter, near the Special Forces hootch, and over the next two weeks they stuck together like a pair of high school steadies. Almost disgusting, Rat said, the way they mooned over each other. Always holding hands, always laughing over some private joke. All they needed, he said, were a couple of matching sweaters. But among the medics there was some envy. This was Vietnam, after all, and Mary Anne Bell was an attractive girl. Too wide in the shoulders, maybe, but she had terrific legs, a bubbly personality, a

happy smile. The men genuinely liked her. Out on the volleyball court she wore cut-off blue jeans and a black swim-
suit top, which the guys appreciated, and in the evenings
she liked to dance to music from Rat's portable tape deck.
There was a novelty to it; she was good for morale. At times
she gave off a kind of come-get-me energy, coy and flirta-
tious, but apparently it never bothered Mark Fossie. In fact
he seemed to enjoy it, just grinning at her, because he was so
much in love, and because it was the sort of show that a girl
will sometimes put on for her boyfriend's entertainment and
education.

Though she was young, Rat said, Mary Anne Bell was no
timid child. She was curious about things. During her first
days in-country she liked to roam around the compound
asking questions: What exactly was a trip flare? How did a
Claymore work? What was behind those scary green mountains to the west? Then she'd squint and listen carefully
while somebody filled her in. She had a good quick mind.
She paid attention. Often, especially during the hot afternoons, she would spend time with the ARVNs out along the
perimeter, picking up little phrases of Vietnamese, learning
how to cook rice over a can of Sterno, how to eat with her
hands. The guys sometimes liked to kid her about it—our
own little native, they'd say—but Mary Anne would just
smile and stick out her tongue. "I'm here," she'd say, "I might
as well learn something."

The war intrigued her. The land, too, and the mystery. At
the beginning of her second week she began pestering Mark
Fossie to take her down to the village at the foot of the hill.
In a quiet voice, very patiently, he tried to tell her that it
was a bad idea, way too dangerous, but Mary Anne kept after him. She wanted to get a feel for how people lived, what

the smells and customs were. It did not impress her that the VC owned the place.

"Listen, it can't be that bad," she said. "They're human beings, aren't they? Like everybody else?"

Fossie nodded. He loved her.

And so in the morning Rat Kiley and two other medics tagged along as security while Mark and Mary Anne strolled through the ville like a pair of tourists. If the girl was nervous, she didn't show it. She seemed comfortable and entirely at home; the hostile atmosphere did not seem to register. All morning Mary Anne chattered away about how quaint the place was, how she loved the thatched roofs and naked children, the wonderful simplicity of village life. A strange thing to watch, Rat said. This seventeen-year-old doll in her goddamn culottes, perky and fresh-faced, like a cheerleader visiting the opposing team's locker room. Her pretty blue eyes seemed to glow. She couldn't get enough of it. On their way back up to the compound she stopped for a swim in the Song Tra Bong, stripping down to her underwear, showing off her legs while Fossie tried to explain to her about things like ambushes and snipers and the stopping power of an AK-47.

The guys, though, were impressed.

"A real tiger," said Eddie Diamond. "D-cup guts, trainer-bra brains."

"She'll learn," somebody said.

Eddie Diamond gave a solemn nod. "There's the scary part. I promise you, this girl will most definitely learn."

In parts, at least, it was a funny story, and yet to hear Rat Kiley tell it you'd almost think it was intended as straight tragedy. He never smiled. Not even at the crazy stuff. There was always a dark, far-off look in his eyes, a kind of sadness, as if he were troubled by something sliding beneath the story's surface. Whenever we laughed, I remember, he'd sigh and wait it out, but the one thing he could not tolerate was disbelief. He'd get edgy if someone questioned one of the details. "She *wasn't* dumb," he'd snap. "I never said that. Young, that's all I said. Like you and me. A *girl*, that's the only difference, and I'll tell you something: it didn't amount to jack. I mean, when we first got here—all of us—we were real young and innocent, full of romantic bullshit, but we learned pretty damn quick. And so did Mary Anne."

Rat would peer down at his hands, silent and thoughtful. After a moment his voice would flatten out.

"You don't believe it?" he'd say. "Fine with me. But you don't know human nature. You don't know Nam."

Then he'd tell us to listen up.

A good sharp mind, Rat said. True, she could be silly sometimes, but she picked up on things fast. At the end of the second week, when four casualties came in, Mary Anne wasn't afraid to get her hands bloody. At times, in fact, she seemed fascinated by it. Not the gore so much, but the adrenaline buzz that went with the job, that quick hot rush in your veins when the choppers settled down and you had to do things fast and right. No time for sorting through options, no thinking at all; you just stuck your hands in and started plugging up holes. She was quiet and steady. She didn't back off from the ugly cases. Over the next day or two, as more casualties trickled in, she learned how to clip an artery and pump up a plastic splint and shoot in morphine. In times of action her face took on a sudden new composure, almost serene, the fuzzy blue eyes narrowing into a tight, intelligent focus. Mark Fossie would grin at this. He was proud, yes, but also amazed. A different person, it seemed, and he wasn't sure what to make of it.

Other things, too. The way she quickly fell into the habits of the bush. No cosmetics, no fingernail filing. She stopped wearing jewelry, cut her hair short and wrapped it in a dark green bandanna. Hygiene became a matter of small consequence. In her second week Eddie Diamond taught her how to disassemble an M-16, how the various parts worked, and from there it was a natural progression to learning how to use the weapon. For hours at a time she plunked away at C-ration cans, a bit unsure of herself, but as it turned out she had a real knack for it. There was a new confidence in her voice, a new authority in the way she carried herself. In many ways she remained naive and immature, still a kid, but Cleveland Heights now seemed very far away.

Once or twice, gently, Mark Fossie suggested that it might be time to think about heading home, but Mary Anne laughed and told him to forget it. "Everything I want," she said, "is right here."

She stroked his arm, and then kissed him.

On one level things remained the same between them. They slept together. They held hands and made plans for after the war. But now there was a new imprecision in the way Mary Anne expressed her thoughts on certain subjects. Not necessarily three kids, she'd say. Not necessarily a house on Lake Erie. "Naturally we'll still get married," she'd tell him, "but it doesn't have to be right away. Maybe travel first. Maybe live together. Just test it out, you know?"

Mark Fossie would nod at this, even smile and agree, but it made him uncomfortable. He couldn't pin it down. Her body seemed foreign somehow—too stiff in places, too firm where the softness used to be. The bubbliness was gone. The nervous giggling, too. When she laughed now, which was rare, it was only when something struck her as truly funny. Her voice seemed to reorganize itself at a lower pitch. In the evenings, while the men played cards, she would sometimes fall into long elastic silences, her eyes fixed on the dark, her arms folded, her foot tapping out a coded message against the floor. When Fossie asked about it one evening, Mary Anne looked at him for a long moment and then shrugged. "It's nothing," she said. "Really nothing. To tell the truth, I've never been happier in my whole life. Never."

Twice, though, she came in late at night. Very late. And then finally she did not come in at all.

Rat Kiley heard about it from Fossie himself. Before dawn one morning, the kid shook him awake. He was in bad shape. His voice seemed hollow and stuffed up, nasal-sounding, as if he had a bad cold. He held a flashlight in his hand, clicking it on and off.

"Mary Anne," he whispered, "I can't *find* her."

Rat sat up and rubbed his face. Even in the dim light it was clear that the boy was in trouble. There were dark smudges under his eyes, the frayed edges of somebody who hadn't slept in a while.

"Gone," Fossie said. "Rat, listen, she's sleeping with somebody. Last night, she didn't even . . . I don't know what to *do*."

Abruptly then, Fossie seemed to collapse. He squatted down, rocking on his heels, still clutching the flashlight. Just a boy—eighteen years old. Tall and blond. A gifted athlete. A nice kid, too, polite and good-hearted, although for the moment none of it seemed to be serving him well.

He kept clicking the flashlight on and off.

"All right, start at the start," Rat said. "Nice and slow. Sleeping with who?"

"I don't know who. Eddie Diamond."

"Eddie?"

"Has to be. The guy's always there, always hanging on her."

Rat shook his head. "Man, I don't know. Can't say it strikes a right note, not with Eddie."

"Yes, but he's—"

"Easy does it," Rat said. He reached out and tapped the boy's shoulder. "Why not just check some bunks? We got nine guys. You and me, that's two, so there's seven possibles. Do a quick body count."

Fossie hesitated. "But I can't . . . If she's there, I mean, if she's with somebody—"

"Oh, Christ."

Rat pushed himself up. He took the flashlight, muttered something, and moved down to the far end of the hootch. For privacy, the men had rigged up curtained walls around their cots, small makeshift bedrooms, and in the dark Rat went quickly from room to room, using the flashlight to pluck out the faces. Eddie Diamond slept a hard deep sleep—the others, too. To be sure, though, Rat checked once more, very carefully, then he reported back to Fossie.

"All accounted for. No extras."

"Eddie?"

"Darvon dreams." Rat switched off the flashlight and tried to think it out. "Maybe she just—I don't know—maybe she camped out tonight. Under the stars or something. You search the compound?"

"Sure I did."

"Well, come on," Rat said. "One more time."

Outside, a soft violet light was spreading out across the eastern hillsides. Two or three ARVN soldiers had built their breakfast fires, but the place was mostly quiet and unmoving. They tried the helipad first, then the mess hall and supply hootches, then they walked the entire six hundred meters of perimeter.

"Okay," Rat finally said. "We got a problem."

When he first told the story, Rat stopped there and looked at Mitchell Sanders for a time.

"So what's your vote? Where was she?"

"The Greenies," Sanders said.

"Yeah?"

Sanders gave him a savvy little smirk. "No other option. That stuff about the Special Forces—how they used the place as a base of operations, how they'd glide in and out —all that had to be there for a *reason*. That's how stories work, man."

Rat thought about it, then shrugged.

"All right, sure, the Greenies. But it's not what Fossie thought. She wasn't sleeping with any of them. At least not exactly. I mean, in a way she was sleeping with *all* of them, more or less, except it wasn't sex or anything. They was just lying together, so to speak, Mary Anne and these six grungy weirded-out Green Berets."

"Lying down?" Sanders said.

"You got it."

"Lying down how?"

Rat smiled. "Ambush. All night long, man, Mary Anne's out on fuckin' *ambush*."

· · ·

Just after sunrise, Rat said, she came trooping in through the wire, tired-looking but cheerful as she dropped her gear and gave Mark Fossie a brisk hug. The six Green Berets did not speak. One of them nodded at her, and the others gave Fossie a long stare, then they filed off to their hootch at the edge of the compound.

"Please," she said. "Not a word."

Fossie took a half step forward and hesitated. It was as though he had trouble recognizing her. She wore a bush hat and filthy green fatigues; she carried the standard M-16 automatic assault rifle; her face was black with charcoal.

Mary Anne handed him the weapon. "I'm exhausted," she said. "We'll talk later."

She glanced over at the Special Forces area, then turned and walked quickly across the compound toward her own bunker. Fossie stood still for a few seconds. A little dazed, it seemed. After a moment, though, he set his jaw and went after her with a hard, fast stride.

"Not later!" he yelled. "Now!"

What happened between them, Rat said, nobody ever knew for sure. But in the mess hall that evening it was clear that an accommodation had been reached. Or more likely, he said, it was a case of setting down some new rules. Mary Anne's hair was freshly shampooed. She wore a white blouse, a navy blue skirt, a pair of plain black flats. Over dinner she kept her eyes down, poking at her food, subdued to the point of silence. Eddie Diamond and some of the others tried to nudge her into talking about the ambush—What was the feeling out there? What exactly did she see and hear?—but the questions seemed to give her trouble. Nervously, she'd look across the table at Fossie. She'd wait a moment, as if to receive some sort of clearance, then she'd bow her head and mumble out a vague word or two. There were no real answers.

Mark Fossie, too, had little to say.

"Nobody's business," he told Rat that night. "One thing for sure, there won't be any more ambushes. No more late nights."

"You laid down the law?"

"Compromise," Fossie said. "I'll put it this way—we're officially engaged."

Rat nodded cautiously.

"Well hey, she'll make a sweet bride," he said. "Combat ready."

Over the next several days there was a strained, tightly wound quality to the way they treated each other, a rigid correctness that was enforced by repetitive acts of will-power. To look at them from a distance, Rat said, you would think they were the happiest two people on the planet. They spent the long afternoons sunbathing together, stretched out side by side on top of their bunker, or playing backgammon in the shade of a giant palm tree, or just sitting quietly. A model of togetherness, it seemed. And yet at close range their faces showed the tension. Too polite, too thoughtful. Mark Fossie tried hard to keep up a self-assured pose, as if nothing had ever come between them, or ever could, but there was a fragility to it, something tentative and false. If Mary Anne happened to move a few steps away from him, even briefly, he'd tighten up and force himself not to watch her. But then a moment later he'd be watching.

In the presence of others, at least, they kept on their masks. Over meals they talked about plans for a huge wedding in Cleveland Heights—a two-day bash, lots of flowers. And yet even then their smiles seemed too intense. They were too quick with their banter; they held hands as if afraid to let go.

It had to end, and eventually it did.

Near the end of the third week Fossie began making arrangements to send her home. At first, Rat said, Mary Anne seemed to accept it, but then after a day or two she fell into a restless gloom, sitting off by herself at the compound's perimeter. Shoulders hunched, her blue eyes opaque, she seemed to disappear inside herself. A couple of times Fossie approached her and tried to talk it out, but Mary Anne just stared out at the dark green mountains to the west. The wilderness seemed to draw her in. A haunted look, Rat said—partly terror, partly rapture. It was as if she had come up on the edge of something, as if she were caught in that no-man's-land between Cleveland Heights and deep jungle. Seventeen years old. Just a child, blond and innocent, but then weren't they all?

The next morning she was gone. The six Greenies were gone, too.

In a way, Rat said, poor Fossie expected it, or something like it, but that did not help much with the pain. The kid couldn't function. The grief took him by the throat and squeezed and would not let go.

"Lost," he kept whispering.

It was nearly three weeks before she returned. But in a sense she never returned. Not entirely, not all of her.

By chance, Rat said, he was awake to see it. A damp misty night, he couldn't sleep, so he'd gone outside for a quick smoke. He was just standing there, he said, watching the moon, and then off to the west a column of silhouettes appeared as if by magic at the margin of the jungle. At first he didn't recognize her—a small, soft shadow among six other shadows. There was no sound. No real substance either. The seven silhouettes seemed to float across the surface of the earth, like spirits, vaporous and unreal. As he watched, Rat said, it made him think of some freaky opium dream. The silhouettes moved without moving. Silently, one by one, they came up the hill, passed through the wire, and drifted in a loose file across the compound. It was then, Rat said, that he picked out Mary Anne's face. Her eyes seemed to shine in the dark—not blue, though, but a bright glowing jungle green. She did not pause at Fossie's bunker. She cradled her weapon and moved swiftly to the Special Forces hootch and followed the others inside.

Briefly, a light came on, and someone laughed, then the place went dark again.

Whenever he told the story, Rat had a tendency to stop now and then, interrupting the flow, inserting little clarifications or bits of analysis and personal opinion. It was a bad habit, Mitchell Sanders said, because all that matters is the raw material, the stuff itself, and you can't clutter it up with your own half-baked commentary. That just breaks the spell. It destroys the magic. What you have to do, Sanders said, is trust your own story. Get the hell out of the way and let it tell itself.

But Rat Kiley couldn't help it. He wanted to bracket the full range of meaning.

"I know it sounds far-out," he'd tell us, "but it's not like *impossible* or anything. We all heard plenty of wackier stories. Some guy comes back from the bush, tells you he saw the Virgin Mary out there, she was riding a goddamn goose or something. Everybody buys it. Everybody smiles and asks how fast was they going, did she have spurs on. Well, it's not like that. This Mary Anne wasn't no virgin but at least she was real. I saw it. When she came in through the wire that night, I was right there, I saw those eyes of hers, I saw how she wasn't even the same person no more. What's so impossible about that? She was a girl, that's all. I mean, if it was a guy, everybody'd say, Hey, no big deal, he got caught up in the Nam shit, he got seduced by the Greenies. See what I mean? You got these blinders on about women. How gentle and peaceful they are. All that crap about how if we had a pussy for president there wouldn't be no more wars. Pure garbage. You got to get rid of that sexist attitude."

Rat would go on like that until Mitchell Sanders couldn't tolerate it any longer. It offended his inner ear.

"The story," Sanders would say. "The whole tone, man, you're wrecking it."

"Tone?"

"The *sound*. You need to get a consistent sound, like slow or fast, funny or sad. All these digressions, they just screw up your story's *sound*. Stick to what happened."

Frowning, Rat would close his eyes.

"Tone?" he'd say. "I didn't know it was all that complicated. The girl joined the zoo. One more animal—end of story."

"Yeah, fine. But tell it right."

At daybreak the next morning, when Mark Fossie heard she was back, he stationed himself outside the fenced-off

Special Forces area. All morning he waited for her, and all afternoon. Around dusk Rat brought him something to eat.

"She has to come out," Fossie said. "Sooner or later, she has to."

"Or else what?" Rat said.

"I go get her. I bring her out."

Rat shook his head. "Your decision. I was you, though, no way I'd mess around with any Greenie types, not for nothing."

"It's Mary Anne in there."

"Sure, I know that. All the same, I'd knock real extra super polite."

Even with the cooling night air Fossie's face was slick with sweat. He looked sick. His eyes were bloodshot; his skin had a whitish, almost colorless cast. For a few minutes Rat waited with him, quietly watching the hootch, then he patted the kid's shoulder and left him alone.

It was after midnight when Rat and Eddie Diamond went out to check on him. The night had gone cold and steamy, a low fog sliding down from the mountains, and out in the dark there was music playing. Not loud but not soft either. It had a chaotic, almost unmusical sound, without rhythm or form or progression, like the noise of nature. A synthesizer, it seemed, or maybe an electric organ. In the background, just audible, a woman's voice was half singing, half chanting, but the lyrics seemed to be in a foreign tongue.

They found Fossie squatting near the gate in front of the Special Forces area. Head bowed, he was swaying to the music, his face wet and shiny. As Eddie bent down beside him, the kid looked up with eyes, not quite in register, ashen and powdery.

"Hear that?" he whispered. "You *hear*? It's Mary Anne."

Eddie Diamond took his arm. "Let's get you inside. Somebody's radio, that's all it is. Move it now."

"Mary Anne. Just listen."

"Sure, but—"

"Listen!"

Fossie suddenly pulled away, twisting sideways, and fell back against the gate. He lay there with his eyes closed. The music—the noise, whatever it was—came from the hootch beyond the fence. The place was dark except for a small glowing window, which stood partly open, the panes dancing in bright reds and yellows as though the glass were on fire. The chanting seemed louder now. Fiercer, too, and higher pitched.

Fossie pushed himself up. He wavered for a moment and then forced the gate open.

"That voice," he said. "Mary Anne."

Rat took a step forward, reaching out for him, but Fossie was already moving fast toward the hootch. He stumbled once, caught himself, and struck the door hard with both arms. There was a noise—a short screeching sound, like a cat—and the door swung in and Fossie was framed there for an instant, his arms stretched out, and then he slipped inside. After a moment Rat and Eddie followed quietly. Just inside the door they found Fossie bent down on one knee. He wasn't moving.

Across the room a dozen candles were burning on the floor near the open window. The place seemed to echo with a deep-wilderness sound—tribal music—bamboo flutes and drums and chimes. But what hit you first, Rat said, was the smell. Two kinds of smells. There was a topmost scent of joss sticks and incense, like the fumes of some exotic smokehouse, but beneath the smoke lay a deeper and much more powerful stench. Impossible to describe, Rat said. It paralyzed your lungs. Thick and numbing, like an animal's den, a mix of blood and scorched hair and excrement and the sweet-sour odor of moldering flesh—the stink of the kill. But that wasn't all. On a post at the rear of the hootch was the decayed head of a large black leopard; strips of yellow-brown skin dangled from the overhead rafters. And bones. Stacks of bones—all kinds. To one side, propped up against a wall, stood a poster in neat black lettering: ASSEMBLE YOUR OWN GOOK!! FREE SAMPLE KIT!! The images came in a swirl, Rat said, and there was no way you could process it all. Off in the gloom a few dim figures lounged in hammocks, or on cots, but none of them moved or spoke. The background music came from a tape deck near the circle of candles, but the high voice was Mary Anne's.

Mark Fossie started to get up but then stiffened.

"Mary Anne?" he said.

Quietly then, she stepped out of the shadows. At least for a moment she seemed to be the same pretty young girl who had arrived a few weeks earlier. She was barefoot. She wore her pink sweater and a white blouse and a simple cotton skirt.

For a long while the girl gazed down at Fossie, almost blankly, and in the candlelight her face had the composure of someone perfectly at peace with herself. It took a few seconds, Rat said, to appreciate the full change. In part it was her eyes: utterly flat and indifferent. There was no emotion in her stare, no sense of the person behind it. But the grotesque part, he said, was her jewelry. At the girl's throat was a necklace of human tongues. Elongated and narrow, like pieces of blackened leather, the tongues were threaded along a length of copper wire, one tongue overlapping the next, the tips curled upward as if caught in a final shrill syllable.

Just for a moment the girl looked at Mark Fossie with something close to contempt.

"There's no sense talking," she said. "I know what you think, but it's not . . . it's not *bad*."

"Bad?" Fossie murmured.

"It's not."

In the shadows there was laughter.

One of the Greenies sat up and lighted a cigar. The others lay silent.

"You're in a place," Mary Anne said softly, "where you don't belong."

She moved her hand in a gesture that encompassed not just the hootch but everything around it, the entire war, the mountains, the mean little villages, the trails and trees and rivers and deep misted-over valleys.

"You just don't *know*," she said. "You hide in this little fortress, behind wire and sandbags, and you don't know . . . Sometimes I want to *eat* this place. The whole country —the dirt, the death—I just want to swallow it and have it there inside me. That's how I feel. It's like this appetite. I get scared sometimes—lots of times—but it's not *bad*. You know? I feel close to myself. When I'm out there at night, I feel close to my own body, I can feel my blood moving, my skin and my fingernails, everything, it's like I'm full of electricity and I'm glowing in the dark—I'm on fire almost —I'm burning away into nothing—but it doesn't matter because I know exactly who I am. You can't feel like that anywhere else."

All this was said without drama, as if to herself, her voice slow and impassive. She was not trying to persuade.

For a few moments she looked at Mark Fossie, who seemed to shrink away, then she turned and moved back into the gloom.

There was nothing to be done.

Rat took Fossie's arm, helped him up, and led him outside. In the darkness there was that flipped-out tribal music, which seemed to come from the earth itself, from the deep rain forest, and a woman's voice rising up in a language beyond translation.

Mark Fossie stood rigid.

"Do something," he whispered. "I can't just let her go like that."

Rat listened for a time, then shook his head.

"Man, you must be deaf. She's already gone."

Rat Kiley stopped there, almost in midsentence, which drove Mitchell Sanders crazy.

"What next?" he said.

"Next?"

"The girl. What happened to her?"

Rat made a small, tired motion with his shoulders. "Hard to tell for sure. Three, four days later I got orders to report here to Alpha Company. Jumped the first chopper out, that's the last I ever seen of the place. Mary Anne, too."

Mitchell Sanders stared at him.

"You can't do that."

"Do what?"

"Jesus Christ, it's against the *rules*," Sanders said. "Against human *nature*. This elaborate story, you can't say, Hey, by the way, I don't know the *ending*. I mean, you got certain obligations."

Rat gave a quick smile. "Okay, man, but up to now, everything I told you is from personal experience, the exact truth. There's a few other things I heard secondhand. Third-hand, actually. From here on it gets to be . . . I don't know what the word is."

"Speculation."

"Yeah, right." Rat looked off to the west, scanning the mountains, as if expecting something to appear on one of the high ridgelines. After a second he shrugged. "Anyhow, maybe two months later I ran into Eddie Diamond over in Bangkok—I was on R&R, just this fluke thing—and he told me some stuff I can't vouch for with my own eyes. Even Eddie didn't really see it. He heard it from one of the Greenies, so you got to take this with a whole shakerful of salt."

Once more, Rat searched the mountains, then he sat back and closed his eyes.

"You know," he said abruptly, "I loved her."

"Say again?"

"A lot. We all did, I guess. The way she looked, Mary Anne made you think about those girls back home, how pure and innocent they all are, how they'll never understand any of this, not in a billion years. Try to tell them about it, they'll just stare at you with those big round candy eyes. They won't understand zip. It's like trying to tell somebody what chocolate tastes like."

Mitchell Sanders nodded. "Or shit."

"There it is, you got to taste it, and that's the thing with Mary Anne. She was *there*. She was up to her eyeballs in it. After the war, man, I promise you, you won't find nobody like her."

Suddenly, Rat pushed up to his feet, moved a few steps away from us, then stopped and stood with his back turned. He was an emotional guy.

"Got hooked, I guess," he said. "I loved her. So when I heard from Eddie about what happened, it almost made me . . . Like you say, it's pure speculation."

"Go on," Mitchell Sanders said. "Finish up."

What happened to her, Rat said, was what happened to all of them. You come over clean and you get dirty and then afterward it's never the same. A question of degree. Some make it intact, some don't make it at all. For Mary Anne Bell, it seemed, Vietnam had the effect of a powerful drug: that mix of unnamed terror and unnamed pleasure that comes as the needle slips in and you know you're risking something. The endorphins start to flow, and the adrenaline, and you hold your breath and creep quietly through the moonlit nightscapes; you become intimate with danger; you're in touch with the far side of yourself, as though it's another hemisphere, and you want to string it out and go wherever the trip takes you and be host to all the possibilities inside yourself. Not *bad*, she'd said. Vietnam made her glow in the dark. She wanted more, she wanted to penetrate deeper into the mystery of herself, and after a time the wanting became needing, which turned then to craving.

According to Eddie Diamond, who heard it from one of the Greenies, she took a greedy pleasure in night patrols. She was good at it; she had the moves. All camouflaged up, her face smooth and vacant, she seemed to flow like water through the dark, like oil, without sound or center. She went barefoot. She stopped carrying a weapon. There were times, apparently, when she took crazy, death-wish chances —things that even the Greenies balked at. It was as if she were taunting some wild creature out in the bush, or in her head, inviting it to show itself, a curious game of hide-and-go-seek that was played out in the dense terrain of a night-mare. She was lost inside herself. On occasion, when they were taken under fire, Mary Anne would stand quietly and watch the tracer rounds snap by, a little smile at her lips, intent on some private transaction with the war. Other times she would simply vanish altogether—for hours, for days.

And then one morning, all alone, Mary Anne walked off into the mountains and did not come back.

No body was ever found. No equipment, no clothing. For all he knew, Rat said, the girl was still alive. Maybe up in one of the high mountain villes, maybe with the Montagnard tribes. But that was guesswork.

There was an inquiry, of course, and a week-long air search, and for a time the Tra Bong compound went crazy with MP and CID types. In the end, however, nothing came of it. It was a war and the war went on. Mark Fossie was busted to PFC, shipped back to a hospital in the States, and two months later received a medical discharge. Mary Anne Bell joined the missing.

But the story did not end there. If you believed the Greenies, Rat said, Mary Anne was still somewhere out there in the dark. Odd movements, odd shapes. Late at night, when the Greenies were out on ambush, the whole rain forest seemed to stare in at them—a watched feeling—and a couple of times they almost saw her sliding through the shadows. Not quite, but almost. She had crossed to the other side. She was part of the land. She was wearing her culottes, her pink sweater, and a necklace of human tongues. She was dangerous. She was ready for the kill.

# Stockings

Henry Dobbins was a good man, and a superb soldier, but sophistication was not his strong suit. The ironies went beyond him. In many ways he was like America itself, big and strong, full of good intentions, a roll of fat jiggling at his belly, slow of foot but always plodding along, always there when you needed him, a believer in the virtues of simplicity and directness and hard labor. Like his country, too, Dobbins was drawn toward sentimentality.

Even now, twenty years later, I can see him wrapping his girlfriend's pantyhose around his neck before heading out on ambush.

It was his one eccentricity. The pantyhose, he said, had the properties of a good-luck charm. He liked putting his nose into the nylon and breathing in the scent of his girl-friend's body; he liked the memories this inspired; he some-times slept with the stockings up against his face, the way an infant sleeps with a flannel blanket, secure and peaceful. More than anything, though, the stockings were a talisman for him. They kept him safe. They gave access to a spiritual world, where things were soft and intimate, a place where he might someday take his girlfriend to live. Like many of us in Vietnam, Dobbins felt the pull of superstition, and he believed firmly and absolutely in the protective power of the stockings. They were like body armor, he thought. Whenever we saddled up for a late-night ambush, putting on our helmets and flak jackets, Henry Dobbins would make a ritual out of arranging the nylons around his neck, carefully tying a knot, draping the two leg sections over his left shoulder. There were some jokes, of course, but we came to appreciate the mystery of it all. Dobbins was invulnerable. Never wounded, never a scratch. In August, he tripped a Bouncing Betty, which failed to detonate. And a week later he got caught in the open during a fierce little firefight, no cover at all, but he just slipped the pantyhose over his nose and breathed deep and let the magic do its work.

It turned us into a platoon of believers. You don't dispute facts.

But then, near the end of October, his girlfriend dumped him. It was a hard blow. Dobbins went quiet for a while, staring down at her letter, then after a time he took out the stockings and tied them around his neck as a comforter.

"No sweat," he said. "The magic doesn't go away."

# Church

One afternoon, somewhere west of the Batangan Peninsula, we came across an abandoned pagoda. Or almost abandoned, because a pair of monks lived there in a tar paper shack, tending a small garden and some broken shrines. They spoke almost no English at all. When we dug our foxholes in the yard, the monks did not seem upset or displeased, though the younger one performed a washing motion with his hands. No one could decide what it meant. The older monk led us into the pagoda. The place was dark and cool, I remember, with crumbling walls and sandbagged windows and a ceiling full of holes. "It's bad news," Kiowa said. "You don't mess with churches." But we spent the night there, turning the pagoda into a little fortress, and then for the next seven or eight days we used the place as a base of operations. It was mostly a very peaceful time. Each morning the two monks brought us buckets of water. They giggled when we stripped down to bathe; they smiled happily while we soaped up and splashed one another. On the second day the older monk carried in a cane chair for the use of Lieutenant Jimmy Cross, placing it near the altar area, bowing and gesturing for him to sit down. The old monk seemed proud of the chair, and proud that such a man as Lieutenant Cross should be sitting in it. On another occasion the younger monk presented us with four ripe watermelons from his garden. He stood watching until the watermelons were eaten down to the rinds, then he smiled and made the strange washing motion with his hands.

Though they were kind to all of us, the monks took a special liking for Henry Dobbins.

"Soldier Jesus," they'd say, "good soldier Jesus."

Squatting quietly in the cool pagoda, they would help Dobbins disassemble and clean his machine gun, carefully brushing the parts with oil. The three of them seemed to have an understanding. Nothing in words, just a quietness they shared.

"You know," Dobbins said to Kiowa one morning, "after the war maybe I'll join up with these guys."

"Join how?" Kiowa said.

"Wear robes. Take the pledge."

Kiowa thought about it. "That's a new one. I didn't know you were all that religious."

"Well, I'm not," Dobbins said. Beside him, the two monks were working on the M-60. He watched them take turns running oiled swabs through the barrel. "I mean, I'm not the churchy type. When I was a little kid, way back, I used to sit there on Sunday counting bricks in the wall. Church wasn't for me. But then in high school, I started to think how I'd like to be a minister. Free house, free car. Lots of potlucks. It looked like a pretty good life."

"You're serious?" Kiowa said.

Dobbins shrugged his shoulders. "What's serious? I was a kid. The thing is, I believed in God and all that, but it wasn't the religious part that interested me. Just being *nice* to people, that's all. Being decent."

"Right," Kiowa said.

"Visit sick people, stuff like that. I would've been good at it, too. Not the brainy part—not sermons and all that—but I'd be okay with the people part."

Henry Dobbins was silent for a time. He smiled at the older monk, who was now cleaning the machine gun's trigger assembly.

"But anyway," Dobbins said, "I couldn't ever be a real minister, because you have to be super sharp. Upstairs, I mean. It takes brains. You have to explain some hard stuff, like why people die, or why God invented pneumonia and all that." He shook his head. "I just didn't have the smarts for it. And there's the religious thing, too. All these years, man, I still hate church."

"Maybe you'd change," Kiowa said.

Henry Dobbins closed his eyes briefly, then laughed.

"One thing for sure, I'd look spiffy in those robes they wear—just like Friar Tuck. Maybe I'll do it. Find a monastery somewhere. Wear a robe and be nice to people."

"Sounds good," Kiowa said.

The two monks were quiet as they cleaned and oiled the machine gun. Though they spoke almost no English, they seemed to have great respect for the conversation, as if sensing that important matters were being discussed. The younger monk used a yellow cloth to wipe dirt from a belt of ammunition.

"What about you?" Dobbins said.

"How?"

"Well, you carry that Bible everywhere, you never hardly swear or anything, so you must—"

"I grew up that way," Kiowa said.

"Did you ever—you know—did you think about being a minister?"

"No. Not ever."

Dobbins laughed. "An Indian preacher. Man, that's one I'd love to see. Feathers and buffalo robes."

Kiowa lay on his back, looking up at the ceiling, and for a time he didn't speak. Then he sat up and took a drink from his canteen.

"Not a minister," he said, "but I do like churches. The way it feels inside. It feels good when you just sit there, like you're in a forest and everything's really quiet, except there's still this sound you can't hear."

"Yeah."

"You ever feel that?"

"Sort of."

Kiowa made a noise in his throat. "This is all wrong," he said.

"What?"

"Setting up here. It's wrong. I don't care what, it's still a church."

Dobbins nodded. "True."

"A church," Kiowa said. "Just wrong."

When the two monks finished cleaning the machine gun, Henry Dobbins began reassembling it, wiping off the excess oil, then he handed each of them a can of peaches and a chocolate bar. "Okay," he said, "*didi mau*, boys. Beat it." The monks bowed and moved out of the pagoda into the bright morning sunlight.

Henry Dobbins made the washing motion with his hands.

"You're right," he said. "All you can do is be nice. Treat them decent, you know?"

# The Man I Killed

His jaw was in his throat, his upper lip and teeth were gone, his one eye was shut, his other eye was a star-shaped hole, his eyebrows were thin and arched like a woman's, his nose was undamaged, there was a slight tear at the lobe of one ear, his clean black hair was swept upward into a cowlick at the rear of the skull, his forehead was lightly freckled, his fingernails were clean, the skin at his left cheek was peeled back in three ragged strips, his right cheek was smooth and hairless, there was a butterfly on his chin, his neck was open to the spinal cord and the blood there was thick and shiny and it was this wound that had killed him. He lay face-up in the center of the trail, a slim, dead, almost dainty young man. He had bony legs, a narrow waist, long shapely fingers. His chest was sunken and poorly muscled—a scholar, maybe. His wrists were the wrists of a child. He wore a black shirt, black pajama pants, a gray ammunition belt, a gold ring on the third finger of his right hand. His rubber sandals had been blown off. One lay beside him, the other a few meters up the trail. He had been born, maybe, in 1946 in the village of My Khe near the central coastline of Quang Ngai Province, where his parents farmed, and where his family had lived for several centuries, and where, during the time of the French, his father and two uncles and many neighbors had joined in the struggle for independence. He was not a Communist. He was a citizen and a soldier. In the village of My Khe, as in all of Quang Ngai, patriotic resistance had the force of tradition, which was partly the force of legend, and from his earliest boyhood the man I killed would have listened to stories about the heroic Trung sisters and Tran Hung Dao's famous rout of the Mongols and Le Loi's final victory against the Chinese at Tot Dong. He would have been taught that to defend the land was a man's highest duty and highest privilege. He had accepted this. It was never open to question. Secretly, though, it also frightened him. He was not a fighter. His health was poor, his body small and frail. He liked books. He wanted someday to be a teacher of mathematics. At night, lying on his mat, he could not picture himself doing the brave things his father had done, or his uncles, or the heroes of the stories. He hoped in his heart that he would never be tested. He hoped the Americans would go away. Soon, he hoped. He kept hoping and hoping, always, even when he was asleep.

"Oh, man, you fuckin' trashed the fucker," Azar said. "You scrambled his sorry self, look at that, you *did*, you laid him out like Shredded fuckin' Wheat."

"Go away," Kiowa said.

"I'm just saying the truth. Like oatmeal."

"Go," Kiowa said.

"Okay, then, I take it back," Azar said. He started to move

away, then stopped and said, "Rice Krispies, you know? On the dead test, this particular individual gets A-plus."

Smiling at this, he shrugged and walked up the trail toward the village behind the trees.

Kiowa kneeled down.

"Just forget that crud," he said. He opened up his canteen and held it out for a while and then sighed and pulled it away. "No sweat, man. What else could you do?"

Later, Kiowa said, "I'm serious. Nothing *anybody* could do. Come on, stop staring."

The trail junction was shaded by a row of trees and tall brush. The slim young man lay with his legs in the shade. His jaw was in his throat. His one eye was shut and the other was a star-shaped hole.

Kiowa glanced at the body.

"All right, let me ask a question," he said. "You want to trade places with him? Turn it all upside down—you *want* that? I mean, be honest."

The star-shaped hole was red and yellow. The yellow part seemed to be getting wider, spreading out at the center of the star. The upper lip and gum and teeth were gone. The man's head was cocked at a wrong angle, as if loose at the neck, and the neck was wet with blood.

"Think it over," Kiowa said.

Then later he said, "Tim, it's a *war*. The guy wasn't Heidi—he had a weapon, right? It's a tough thing, for sure, but you got to cut out that staring."

Then he said, "Maybe you better lie down a minute."

Then after a long empty time he said, "Take it slow. Just go wherever the spirit takes you."

The butterfly was making its way along the young man's

forehead, which was spotted with small dark freckles. The nose was undamaged. The skin on the right cheek was smooth and fine-grained and hairless. Frail-looking, delicately boned, the young man would not have wanted to be a soldier and in his heart would have feared performing badly in battle. Even as a boy growing up in the village of My Khe, he had often worried about this. He imagined covering his head and lying in a deep hole and closing his eyes and not moving until the war was over. He had no stomach for violence. He loved mathematics. His eyebrows were thin and arched like a woman's, and at school the boys sometimes teased him about how pretty he was, the arched eyebrows and long shapely fingers, and on the playground they mimicked a woman's walk and made fun of his smooth skin and his love for mathematics. The young man could not make himself fight them. He often wanted to, but he was afraid, and this increased his shame. If he could not fight little boys, he thought, how could he ever become a soldier and fight the Americans with their airplanes and helicopters and bombs? It did not seem possible. In the presence of his father and uncles, he pretended to look forward to doing his patriotic duty, which was also a privilege, but at night he prayed with his mother that the war might end soon. Beyond anything else, he was afraid of disgracing himself, and therefore his family and village. But all he could do, he thought, was wait and pray and try not to grow up too fast.

"Listen to me," Kiowa said. "You feel terrible, I know that."

Then he said, "Okay, maybe I don't know."

Along the trail there were small blue flowers shaped like bells. The young man's head was wrenched sideways, not quite facing the flowers, and even in the shade a single blade of sunlight sparkled against the buckle of his ammunition belt. The left cheek was peeled back in three ragged strips. The wounds at his neck had not yet clotted, which made him seem animate even in death, the blood still spreading out across his shirt.

Kiowa shook his head.

There was some silence before he said, "Stop *staring.*"

The young man's fingernails were clean. There was a slight tear at the lobe of one ear, a sprinkling of blood on the forearm. He wore a gold ring on the third finger of his right hand. His chest was sunken and poorly muscled—a scholar, maybe. His life was now a constellation of possibilities. So, yes, maybe a scholar. And for years, despite his family's poverty, the man I killed would have been determined to continue his education in mathematics. The means for this were arranged, perhaps, through the village liberation cadres, and in 1964 the young man began attending classes at the university in Saigon, where he avoided politics and paid attention to the problems of calculus. He devoted himself to his studies. He spent his nights alone, wrote romantic poems in his journal, took pleasure in the grace and beauty of differential equations. The war, he knew, would finally take him, but for the time being he would not let himself think about it. He had stopped praying; instead, now, he waited. And as he waited, in his final year at the university, he fell in love with a classmate, a girl of seventeen, who one day told him that his wrists were like the wrists of a child, so small and delicate, and who admired his narrow waist and the cowlick that rose up like a bird's tail at the back of his head. She liked his quiet manner; she laughed at his freckles and bony legs. One evening, perhaps, they exchanged gold rings.

Now one eye was a star.

"You okay?" Kiowa said.

The corpse lay almost entirely in shade. There were gnats at the mouth, little flecks of pollen drifting above the nose. The butterfly was gone. The bleeding had stopped except for the neck wounds.

Kiowa picked up the rubber sandals, clapping off the dirt, then bent down to search the body. He found a pouch of rice, a comb, a fingernail clipper, a few soiled piasters, a snapshot of a young woman standing in front of a parked motorcycle. Kiowa placed these items in his rucksack along with the gray ammunition belt and rubber sandals.

Then he squatted down.

"I'll tell you the straight truth," he said. "The guy was dead the second he stepped on the trail. Understand me? We all had him zeroed. A good kill—weapon, ammunition, everything." Tiny beads of sweat glistened at Kiowa's forehead. His eyes moved from the sky to the dead man's body to the knuckles of his own hands. "So listen, you best pull your shit together. Can't just sit here all day."

Later he said, "Understand?"

Then he said, "Five minutes, Tim. Five more minutes and we're moving out."

The one eye did a funny twinkling trick, red to yellow. His head was wrenched sideways, as if loose at the neck, and the dead young man seemed to be staring at some distant object beyond the bell-shaped flowers along the trail. The blood at the neck had gone to a deep purplish black. Clean fingernails, clean hair—he had been a soldier for only a single day. After his years at the university, the man I killed returned with his new wife to the village of My Khe, where he enlisted as a common rifleman with the 48th Vietcong Battalion. He knew he would die quickly. He knew he would see a flash of light. He knew he would fall dead and wake up in the stories of his village and people.

Kiowa covered the body with a poncho.

"Hey, you're looking better," he said. "No doubt about it. All you needed was time—some mental R&R."

Then he said, "Man, I'm sorry."

Then later he said, "Why not talk about it?"

Then he said, "Come on, man, talk."

He was a slim, dead, almost dainty young man of about twenty. He lay with one leg bent beneath him, his jaw in his throat, his face neither expressive nor inexpressive. One eye was shut. The other was a star-shaped hole.

"Talk," Kiowa said.

# Ambush

When she was nine, my daughter Kathleen asked if I had ever killed anyone. She knew about the war; she knew I'd been a soldier. "You keep writing these war stories," she said, "so I guess you must've killed somebody." It was a difficult moment, but I did what seemed right, which was to say, "Of course not," and then to take her onto my lap and hold her for a while. Someday, I hope, she'll ask again. But here I want to pretend she's a grown-up. I want to tell her exactly what happened, or what I remember happening, and then I want to say to her that as a little girl she was absolutely right. This is why I keep writing war stories:

He was a short, slender young man of about twenty. I was afraid of him—afraid of something—and as he passed me on the trail I threw a grenade that exploded at his feet and killed him.

Or to go back:

Shortly after midnight we moved into the ambush site outside My Khe. The whole platoon was there, spread out in the dense brush along the trail, and for five hours nothing at all happened. We were working in two-man teams—one man on guard while the other slept, switching off every two hours—and I remember it was still dark when Kiowa shook me awake for the final watch. The night was foggy and hot. For the first few moments I felt lost, not sure about directions, groping for my helmet and weapon. I reached out and found three grenades and lined them up in front of me; the pins had already been straightened for quick throwing. And then for maybe half an hour I kneeled there and waited. Very gradually, in tiny slivers, dawn began to break through the fog, and from my position in the brush I could see ten or fifteen meters up the trail. The mosquitoes were fierce. I remember slapping at them, wondering if I should wake up Kiowa and ask for some repellent, then thinking it was a bad idea, then looking up and seeing the young man come out of the fog. He wore black clothing and rubber sandals and a gray ammunition belt. His shoulders were slightly stooped, his head cocked to the side as if listening for something. He seemed at ease. He carried his weapon in one hand, muzzle down, moving without any hurry up the center of the trail. There was no sound at all—none that I can remember. In a way, it seemed, he was part of the morning fog, or my own imagination, but there was also the reality of what was happening in my stomach. I had already pulled the pin on a grenade. I had come up to a crouch. It was entirely automatic. I did not hate the young man; I did not see him as the enemy; I did not ponder issues of morality or politics or military duty. I crouched and kept my head low. I tried to swallow whatever was rising from my stomach, which tasted like lemonade, something fruity and sour. I was terrified. There were no thoughts about killing. The grenade was to make him go away—just evaporate—and I leaned back and felt my head go empty and then felt it fill up again. I had already thrown the grenade before telling myself to throw it. The brush was thick and I had to lob it high, not aiming, and I remember the grenade seeming to freeze above me for an instant, as if a camera had clicked, and I remember ducking down and holding my breath and seeing little wisps of fog rise from the earth. The grenade bounced once and rolled across the trail. I did not hear it, but there must've been a sound, because the young man dropped his weapon and began to run, just two or three quick steps, then he hesitated, swiveling to his right, and he glanced down at the grenade and tried to cover his head but never did. It occurred to me then that he was about to die. I wanted to warn him. The grenade made a popping noise—not soft but not loud either—not what I'd expected—and there was a puff of dust and smoke—a small white puff—and the young man seemed to jerk upward as if pulled by invisible wires. He fell on his back. His rubber sandals had been blown off. He lay at the center of the trail, his right leg bent beneath him, his one eye shut, his other eye a huge star-shaped hole.

For me, it was not a matter of live or die. I was in no real peril. Almost certainly the young man would have passed me by. And it will always be that way.

Later, I remember, Kiowa tried to tell me that the man would've died anyway. He told me that it was a good kill, that I was a soldier and this was a war, that I should shape up and stop staring and ask myself what the dead man would've done if things were reversed.

None of it mattered. The words seemed far too complicated. All I could do was gape at the fact of the young man's body.

Even now I haven't finished sorting it out. Sometimes I forgive myself, other times I don't. In the ordinary hours of life I try not to dwell on it, but now and then, when I'm reading a newspaper or just sitting alone in a room, I'll look up and see the young man step out of the morning fog. I'll watch him walk toward me, his shoulders slightly stooped, his head cocked to the side, and he'll pass within a few yards of me and suddenly smile at some secret thought and then continue up the trail to where it bends back into the fog.

# Style

There was no music. Most of the hamlet had burned down, including her house, which was now smoke, and the girl danced with her eyes half closed, her feet bare. She was maybe fourteen. She had black hair and brown skin. "Why's she dancing?" Azar said. We searched through the wreckage but there wasn't much to find. Rat Kiley caught a chicken for dinner. Lieutenant Cross radioed up to the gunships and told them to go away. The girl danced mostly on her toes. She took tiny steps in the dirt in front of her house, sometimes making a slow twirl, sometimes smiling to herself. "Why's she dancing?" Azar said, and Henry Dobbins said it didn't matter why, she just was. Later we found her family in the house. They were dead and badly burned. It wasn't a big family: an infant and an old woman and a woman whose age was hard to tell. When we dragged them out, the girl kept dancing. She put the palms of her hands against her ears, which must've meant something, and she danced sideways for a short while, and then backwards.

She did a graceful movement with her hips. "Well, I don't get it," Azar said. The smoke from the hootches smelled like straw. It moved in patches across the village square, not thick anymore, sometimes just faint ripples like fog. There were dead pigs, too. The girl went up on her toes and made a slow turn and danced through the smoke. Her face had a dreamy look, quiet and composed. A while later, when we moved out of the hamlet, she was still dancing. "Probably some weird ritual," Azar said, but Henry Dobbins looked back and said no, the girl just liked to dance.

That night, after we'd marched away from the smoking village, Azar mocked the girl's dancing. He did funny jumps and spins. He put the palms of his hands against his ears and danced sideways for a while, and then backwards, and then did an erotic thing with his hips. But Henry Dobbins, who moved gracefully for such a big man, took Azar from behind and lifted him up high and carried him over to a deep well and asked if he wanted to be dumped in.

Azar said no.

"All right, then," Henry Dobbins said, "dance right."

# Speaking of Courage

The war was over and there was no place in particular to go. Norman Bowker followed the tar road on its seven-mile loop around the lake, then he started all over again, driving slowly, feeling safe inside his father's big Chevy, now and then looking out on the lake to watch the boats and water-skiers and scenery. It was Sunday and it was summer, and the town seemed pretty much the same. The lake lay flat and silvery against the sun. Along the road the houses were all low-slung and split-level and modern, with big porches and picture windows facing the water. The lawns were spacious. On the lake side of the road, where real estate was most valuable, the houses were handsome and set deep in, well kept and brightly painted, with docks jutting out into the lake, and boats moored and covered with canvas, and neat gardens, and sometimes even gardeners, and stone patios with barbecue spits and grills, and wooden shingles saying who lived where. On the other side of the road, to his left, the houses were also handsome, though less expensive and on a smaller scale and with no docks or boats or gardeners. The road was a sort of boundary between the affluent and the almost affluent, and to live on the lake side of the road was one of the few natural privileges in a town of the prairie—the difference between watching the sun set over cornfields or over water.

It was a graceful, good-sized lake. Back in high school, at night, he had driven around and around it with Sally Kramer, wondering if she'd want to pull into the shelter of Sunset Park, or other times with his friends, talking about urgent matters, worrying about the existence of God and theories of causation. Then, there had not been a war. But there had always been the lake, which was the town's first cause of existence, a place for immigrant settlers to put down their loads. Before the settlers were the Sioux, and before the Sioux were the vast open prairies, and before the prairies there was only ice. The lake bed had been dug out by the southernmost advance of the Wisconsin glacier. Fed by neither streams nor springs, the lake was often filthy and algaed, relying on fickle prairie rains for replenishment. Still, it was the only important body of water within forty miles, a source of pride, nice to look at on bright summer days, and later that evening it would color up with fireworks. Now, in the late afternoon, it lay calm and smooth, a good audience for silence, a seven-mile circumference that could be traveled by slow car in twenty-five minutes. It was not such a good lake for swimming. After high school, he'd caught an ear infection that had almost kept him out of the war. And the lake had drowned his friend Max Arnold, keeping him out of the war entirely. Max had been one who liked to talk about the existence of God. "No, I'm not saying *that*," he'd argue against the drone of the engine. "I'm saying it's possible as an *idea*, even necessary as an idea, a final cause in the whole structure of causation." Now he knew, perhaps. Before the war, they'd driven around the lake as friends, but now Max was just an idea, and most of Norman Bowker's other friends were living in Des Moines or Sioux City, or going to school somewhere, or holding down jobs. The high school girls were mostly gone or married. Sally Kramer, whose pictures he had once carried in his wallet, was one who had married. Her name was now Sally Gustafson and she lived in a pleasant blue house on the less expensive side of the lake road. On his third day home he'd seen her out mowing the lawn, still pretty in a lacy red blouse and white shorts. For a moment he'd almost pulled over, just to talk, but instead he'd pushed down hard on the gas pedal. She looked happy. She had her house and her new husband, and there was really nothing he could say to her.

The town seemed remote somehow. Sally was married and Max was drowned and his father was at home watching baseball on national TV.

Norman Bowker shrugged. "No problem," he murmured.

Clockwise, as if in orbit, he took the Chevy on another seven-mile turn around the lake.

Even in late afternoon the day was hot. He turned on the air conditioner, then the radio, and he leaned back and let the cold air and music blow over him. Along the road, kicking stones in front of them, two young boys were hiking with knapsacks and toy rifles and canteens. He honked going by, but neither boy looked up. Already he had passed them six times, forty-two miles, nearly three hours without stop. He watched the boys recede in his rearview mirror. They turned a soft brownish color, like sand, before finally disappearing.

He tapped down lightly on the accelerator.

Out on the lake a man's motorboat had stalled; the man was bent over the engine with a wrench and a frown. Beyond the stalled boat there were other boats, and a few water-skiers, and the smooth July waters, and an immense flatness everywhere. Two mud hens floated stiffly beside a white dock.

The road curved west, where the sun had now dipped low. He figured it was close to five o'clock—twenty after, he guessed. The war had taught him to tell time without clocks, and even at night, waking from sleep, he could usually place it within ten minutes either way. What he should do, he thought, is stop at Sally's house and impress her with this new time-telling trick of his. They'd talk for a while, catching up on things, and then he'd say, "Well, better hit the road, it's five thirty-four," and she'd glance at her wristwatch and say, "Hey! How'd you *do* that?" and he'd give a casual shrug and tell her it was just one of those things you pick up. He'd keep it light. He wouldn't say anything about anything. "How's it being married?" he might ask, and he'd nod at whatever she answered with, and he would not say a word about how he'd almost won the Silver Star for valor.

He drove past Slater Park and across the causeway and past Sunset Park. The radio announcer sounded tired. The temperature in Des Moines was eighty-one degrees, and the time was five thirty-five, and "All you on the road, drive extra careful now on this fine Fourth of July." If Sally had not been married, or if his father were not such a baseball fan, it would have been a good time to talk.

"The Silver Star?" his father might have said.

"Yes, but I didn't get it. Almost, but not quite."

And his father would have nodded, knowing full well that many brave men do not win medals for their bravery, and that others win medals for doing nothing. As a starting point, maybe, Norman Bowker might then have listed the seven medals he did win: the Combat Infantryman's Badge, the Air Medal, the Army Commendation Medal, the Good Conduct Medal, the Vietnam Campaign Medal, the Bronze Star, and the Purple Heart, though his wound was minor and did not leave a scar and did not hurt and never had. He would've explained to his father that none of these decorations was for uncommon valor. They were for common valor. The routine, daily stuff—just humping, just enduring—but that was worth something, wasn't it? Yes, it was. Worth plenty. The ribbons looked good on the uniform in his closet, and if his father were to ask, he would've explained what each signified and how he was proud of all of them, especially the Combat Infantryman's Badge, because it meant he had been there as a real soldier and had done all the things soldiers do, and therefore it wasn't such a big deal that he could not bring himself to be uncommonly brave.

And then he would have talked about the medal he did not win and why he did not win it.

"I almost won the Silver Star," he would have said.

"How's that?"

"Just a story."

"So tell me," his father would have said.

Slowly then, circling the lake, Norman Bowker would have started by describing the Song Tra Bong. "A river," he would've said, "this slow flat muddy river." He would've explained how during the dry season it was exactly like any other river, nothing special, but how in October the monsoons began and the whole situation changed. For a solid week the rains never stopped, not once, and so after a few days the Song Tra Bong overflowed its banks and the land turned into a deep, thick muck for a quarter mile on either side. Just muck—no other word for it. Like quicksand, almost, except the stink was incredible. "You couldn't even sleep," he'd tell his father. "At night you'd find a high spot, and you'd doze off, but then later you'd wake up because you'd be buried in all that slime. You'd just sink in. You'd feel it ooze up over your body and sort of suck you down. And the whole time there was that constant rain. I mean, it never stopped, not ever."

"Sounds pretty wet," his father would've said, pausing briefly. "So what happened?"

"You really want to hear this?"

"Hey, I'm your *father*."

Norman Bowker smiled. He looked out across the lake and imagined the feel of his tongue against the truth. "Well, this one time, this one night out by the river . . . I wasn't very brave."

"You have seven medals."

"Sure."

"Seven. Count 'em. You weren't a coward either."

"Well, maybe not. But I had the chance and I blew it. The stink, that's what got to me. I couldn't take that goddamn awful *smell*."

"If you don't want to say more—"

"I do want to."

"All right then. Slow and sweet, take your time."

The road descended into the outskirts of town, turning northwest past the junior college and the tennis courts, then past Chautauqua Park, where the picnic tables were spread with sheets of colored plastic and where picnickers sat in lawn chairs and listened to the high school band playing Sousa marches under the band shell. The music faded after a few blocks. He drove beneath a canopy of elms, then along a stretch of open shore, then past the municipal docks, where a woman in pedal pushers stood casting for bullheads. There were no other fish in the lake except for perch and a few worthless carp. It was a bad lake for swimming and fishing both.

He drove slowly. No hurry, nowhere to go. Inside the Chevy the air was cool and oily-smelling, and he took pleasure in the steady sounds of the engine and air-conditioning. A tour bus feeling, in a way, except the town he was touring seemed dead. Through the windows, as if in a stop-motion photograph, the place looked as if it had been hit by nerve gas, everything still and lifeless, even the people. The town could not talk, and would not listen. "How'd you like to hear about the war?" he might have asked, but the place could only blink and shrug. It had no memory, therefore no guilt. The taxes got paid and the votes got counted and the agencies of government did their work briskly and politely. It was a brisk, polite town. It did not know shit about shit, and did not care to know.

Norman Bowker leaned back and considered what he might've said on the subject. He knew shit. It was his specialty. The smell, in particular, but also the numerous varieties of texture and taste. Someday he'd give a lecture on the topic. Put on a suit and tie and stand up in front of the Ki-

wanis club and tell the fuckers about all the wonderful shit
he knew. Pass out samples, maybe.

Smiling at this, he clamped the steering wheel slightly
right of center, which produced a smooth clockwise motion
against the curve of the road. The Chevy seemed to know its
own way.

The sun was lower now. Five fifty-five, he decided—six
o'clock, tops.

Along an unused railway spur, four workmen labored
in the shadowy red heat, setting up a platform and steel
launchers for the evening fireworks. They were dressed alike
in khaki trousers, work shirts, visored caps, and brown boots.
Their faces were dark and smudgy. "Want to hear about the
Silver Star I almost won?" Norman Bowker whispered, but
none of the workmen looked up. Later they would blow
color into the sky. The lake would sparkle with reds and
blues and greens, like a mirror, and the picnickers would
make low sounds of appreciation.

"Well, see, it never stopped raining," he would've said.
"The muck was everywhere, you couldn't get away from it."

He would have paused a second.

Then he would have told about the night they biv-
ouacked in a field along the Song Tra Bong. A big swampy
field beside the river. There was a ville nearby, fifty meters
downstream, and right away a dozen old mama-sans ran
out and started yelling. A crazy scene, he would've said. The
mama-sans just stood there in the rain, soaking wet, yap-
ping away about how this field was bad news. Number ten,
they said. Evil ground. Not a good spot for good GIs. Finally
Lieutenant Jimmy Cross had to get out his pistol and fire off
a few rounds just to shoo them away. By then it was almost

dark. So they set up a perimeter, ate chow, then crawled un-der their ponchos and tried to settle in for the night.

But the rain kept getting worse. And by midnight the field turned into soup.

"Just this deep, oozy soup," he would've said. "Like sew-age or something. Thick and mushy. You couldn't sleep. You couldn't even lie down, not for long, because you'd start to sink under the soup. Real clammy. You could feel the crud coming up inside your boots and pants."

Here, Norman Bowker would have squinted against the low sun. He would have kept his voice cool, no self-pity.

"But the worst part," he would've said quietly, "was the smell. Partly it was the river—a dead-fish smell—but it was something else, too. Finally somebody figured it out. What this was, it was a shit field. The village toilet. No indoor plumbing, right? So they used the field. I mean, we were camped in a goddamn *shit* field."

He imagined Sally Kramer closing her eyes.

If she were here with him, in the car, she would've said, "Stop it. I don't like that word."

"That's what it *was.*"

"All right, but you don't have to use that word."

"Fine. What should we call it?"

She would have glared at him. "I don't know. Just stop it."

Clearly, he thought, this was not a story for Sally Kra-mer. She was Sally Gustafson now. No doubt Max would've liked it, the irony in particular, but Max had become a pure idea, which was its own irony. It was just too bad. If his fa-ther were here, riding shotgun around the lake, the old man might have glanced over for a second, understanding per-fectly well that it was not a question of offensive language but of fact. His father would have sighed and folded his arms and waited.

"A shit field," Norman Bowker would have said. "And later that night I could've won the Silver Star for valor."

"Right," his father would've murmured, "I hear you."

The Chevy rolled smoothly across a viaduct and up the narrow tar road. To the right was open lake. To the left, across the road, most of the lawns were scorched dry like October corn. Hopelessly, round and round, a rotating sprinkler scattered lake water on Dr. Mason's vegetable garden. Already the prairie had been baked dry, but in August it would get worse. The lake would turn green with algae, and the golf course would burn up, and the dragonflies would crack open for want of good water.

The big Chevy curved past Centennial Beach and the A&W root beer stand.

It was his eighth revolution around the lake.

He followed the road past the handsome houses with their docks and wooden shingles. Back to Slater Park, across the causeway, around to Sunset Park, as though riding on tracks.

The two little boys were still trudging along on their seven-mile hike.

Out on the lake, the man in the stalled motorboat still fiddled with his engine. The pair of mud hens floated like wooden decoys, and the water-skiers looked tanned and athletic, and the high school band was packing up its instruments, and the woman in pedal pushers patiently rebaited her hook for another try.

Quaint, he thought.

A hot summer day and it was all very quaint and remote.

The four workmen had almost completed their preparations for the evening fireworks.

Facing the sun again, Norman Bowker decided it was nearly seven o'clock. Not much later the tired radio announcer confirmed it, his voice rocking itself into a deep Sunday snooze. If Max Arnold were here, he would say something about the announcer's fatigue, and relate it to the bright pink in the sky, and the war, and courage. A pity that Max was gone. And a pity about his father, who had his own war and who now preferred silence.

Still, there was so much to say.

How the rain never stopped. How the cold worked into your bones. Sometimes the bravest thing on earth was to sit through the night and feel the cold in your bones. Courage was not always a matter of yes or no. Sometimes it came in degrees, like the cold; sometimes you were very brave up to a point and then beyond that point you were not so brave. In certain situations you could do incredible things, you could advance toward enemy fire, but in other situations, which were not nearly so bad, you had trouble keeping your eyes open. Sometimes, like that night in the shit field, the difference between courage and cowardice was something small and stupid.

The way the earth bubbled. And the smell.

In a soft voice, without flourishes, he would have told the exact truth.

"Late in the night," he would've said, "we took some mortar fire."

He would've explained how it was still raining, and how the clouds were pasted to the field, and how the mortar rounds seemed to come right out of the clouds. Everything

was black and wet. The field just exploded. Rain and slop
and shrapnel, nowhere to run, and all they could do was
worm down into slime and cover up and wait. He would've
described the crazy things he saw. Unnatural things. Like
how at one point he noticed a guy lying next to him in the
sludge, completely buried except for his face, and how after a moment the guy rolled his eyes and winked at him.
The noise was fierce. Heavy thunder, and mortar rounds, and
people yelling. Some of the men began shooting up flares.
Red and green and silver flares, all colors, and the rain came
down in Technicolor.

The field was boiling. The shells made deep slushy craters, opening up all those years of waste, centuries worth,
and the smell came bubbling out of the earth. Two rounds
hit close by. Then a third, even closer, and immediately, off
to his left, he heard somebody screaming. It was Kiowa—he
knew that. The sound was ragged and clotted up, but even
so he knew the voice. A strange gargling noise. Rolling sideways, he crawled toward the screaming in the dark. The rain
was hard and steady. Along the perimeter there were quick
bursts of gunfire. Another round hit nearby, spraying up
shit and water, and for a few moments he ducked down beneath the mud. He heard the valves in his heart. He heard
the quick, feathering action of the hinges. Extraordinary, he
thought. As he came up, a pair of red flares puffed open, a
soft blurry glow, and in the glow he saw Kiowa's wide-open
eyes settling down into the scum. All he could do was watch.
He heard himself moan. Then he moved again, crabbing forward, but when he got there Kiowa was almost completely
under. There was a knee. There was an arm and a gold wristwatch and part of a boot.

He could not describe what happened next, not ever, but he would've tried anyway. He would've spoken carefully so as to make it real for anyone who would listen.

There were bubbles where Kiowa's head should've been.

The left hand was curled open; the fingers were filthy; the wristwatch gave off a green phosphorescent shine as it slipped beneath the thick waters.

He would've talked about this, and how he grabbed Kiowa by the boot and tried to pull him out. He pulled hard but Kiowa was gone, and then suddenly he felt himself going, too. The shit was in his nose and eyes. There were flares and mortar rounds, and the stink was everywhere—it was inside him, in his lungs—and he could no longer tolerate it. Not here, he thought. Not like this. He released Kiowa's boot and watched it slide away. Slowly, working his way up, he hoisted himself out of the deep mud, and then he lay still and tasted the shit in his mouth and closed his eyes and listened to the rain and explosions and bubbling sounds.

He was alone.

He had lost his weapon but it didn't matter. All he wanted was a bath.

Nothing else. A hot soapy bath.

Circling the lake, Norman Bowker remembered how his friend Kiowa had disappeared under the waste and water.

"I didn't flip out," he would've said. "I was cool. If things had gone right, if it hadn't been for that smell, I could've won the Silver Star."

A good war story, he thought, but it was not a war for war stories, nor for talk of valor, and nobody in town wanted to know about the terrible stink. They wanted good intentions and good deeds. But the town was not to blame, really.

It was a nice little town, very prosperous, with neat houses and all the sanitary conveniences.

Norman Bowker lit a cigarette and cranked open his window. Seven thirty-five, he decided.

The lake had divided into two halves. One half still glistened, the other was caught in shadow. Along the causeway, the two little boys marched on. The man in the stalled motorboat yanked frantically on the cord to his engine, and the two mud hens sought supper at the bottom of the lake, tails bobbing. He passed Sunset Park once again, and more houses, and the junior college and the tennis courts, and the picnickers, who now sat waiting for the evening fireworks. The high school band was gone. The woman in pedal pushers patiently toyed with her line.

Although it was not yet dusk, the A&W was already awash in neon lights.

He maneuvered his father's Chevy into one of the parking slots, let the engine idle, and sat back. The place was doing a good holiday business. Mostly kids, it seemed, and a few farmers in for the day. He did not recognize any of the faces. A slim, hipless young carhop passed by, but when he hit the horn, she did not seem to notice. Her eyes slid sideways. She hooked a tray to the window of a Firebird, laughing lightly, leaning forward to chat with the three boys inside.

He felt invisible in the soft twilight. Straight ahead, over the take-out counter, swarms of mosquitoes electrocuted themselves against an aluminum Pest-Rid machine.

It was a calm, quiet summer evening.

He honked again, this time leaning on the horn. The young carhop turned slowly, as if puzzled, then said something to the boys in the Firebird and moved reluctantly toward him. Pinned to her shirt was a badge that said EAT MAMA BURGERS.

When she reached his window, she stood straight up so that all he could see was the badge.

"Mama Burger," he said. "Maybe some fries, too."

The girl sighed, leaned down, and shook her head. Her eyes were as fluffy and airy-light as cotton candy.

"You blind?" she said.

She put out her hand and tapped an intercom attached to a steel post.

"Punch the button and place your order. All I do is carry the dumb trays."

She stared at him for a moment. Briefly, he thought, a question lingered in her fuzzy eyes, but then she turned and punched the button for him and returned to her friends in the Firebird.

The intercom squeaked and said, "Order."

"Mama Burger and fries," Norman Bowker said.

"Affirmative, copy clear. No rootie-tootie?"

"Rootie-tootie?"

"You know, man — *root* beer."

"A small one."

"Roger-dodger. Repeat: one Mama, one fries, one small beer. Fire for effect. Stand by."

The intercom squeaked and went dead.

"Out," said Norman Bowker.

When the girl brought his tray, he ate quickly, without looking up. The tired radio announcer in Des Moines gave the time, almost eight-thirty. Dark was pressing in tight now, and he wished there were somewhere to go. In the morning he'd check out job possibilities. Shoot a few buckets down at the Y, maybe wash the Chevy.

He finished his root beer and pushed the intercom button.

"Order," said the tinny voice.

"All done."

"That's it?"

"I guess so."

"Hey, loosen up," the voice said. "What you really need, friend?"

Norman Bowker smiled.

"Well," he said, "how'd you like to hear about—"

He stopped and shook his head.

"Hear *what*, man?"

"Nothing."

"Well, hey," the intercom said, "I'm sure as fuck not *going* anywhere. Screwed to a post, for God sake. Go ahead, try me."

"Nothing."

"You sure?"

"Positive. All done."

The intercom made a light sound of disappointment. "Your choice, I guess. Over an' out."

"Out," said Norman Bowker.

On his tenth turn around the lake he passed the hiking boys for the last time. The man in the stalled motorboat was gone; the mud hens were gone. Beyond the lake, over Sally Gustafson's house, the sun had left a smudge of purple on the horizon. The band shell was deserted, and the woman in pedal pushers quietly reeled in her line, and Dr. Mason's sprinkler went round and round.

On his eleventh revolution he switched off the air-conditioning, opened up his window, and rested his elbow comfortably on the sill, driving with one hand.

There was nothing to say.

He could not talk about it and never would. The evening was smooth and warm.

If it had been possible, which it wasn't, he would have explained how his friend Kiowa slipped away that night beneath the dark swampy field. He was folded in with the war; he was part of the waste.

Turning on his headlights, driving slowly, Norman Bowker remembered how he had taken hold of Kiowa's boot and pulled hard, but how the smell was simply too much, and how he'd backed off and in that way had lost the Silver Star.

He wished he could've explained some of this. How he had been braver than he ever thought possible, but how he had not been so brave as he wanted to be. The distinction was important. Max Arnold, who loved fine lines, would've appreciated it. And his father, who already knew, would've nodded.

"The truth," Norman Bowker would've said, "is I let the guy go."

"Maybe he was already gone."

"He wasn't."

"But maybe."

"No, I could feel it. He wasn't. Some things you can feel."

His father would have been quiet for a while, watching the headlights against the narrow tar road.

"Well, anyway," the old man would've said, "there's still the seven medals."

"I suppose."

"Seven honeys."

"Right."

On his twelfth revolution, the sky went crazy with color.

He pulled into Sunset Park and stopped in the shadow of a picnic shelter. After a time he got out, walked down to the beach, and waded into the lake without undressing. The water felt warm against his skin. He put his head under. He opened his lips, very slightly, for the taste, then he stood up and folded his arms and watched the fireworks. For a small town, he decided, it was a pretty good show.

# Notes

S peaking of Courage" was written in 1975 at the
suggestion of Norman Bowker, who three years
later hanged himself in the locker room of a YMCA in his
hometown in central Iowa.

In the spring of 1975, near the time of Saigon's final collapse, I received a long, disjointed letter in which Bowker
described the problem of finding a meaningful use for his
life after the war. He had worked briefly as an automotive
parts salesman, a janitor, a car wash attendant, and a short-
order cook at the local A&W fast-food franchise. None of
these jobs, he said, had lasted more than ten weeks. He lived
with his parents, who supported him, and who treated him
with kindness and obvious love. At one point he had en-
rolled in the junior college in his hometown, but the course
work, he said, seemed too abstract, too distant, with nothing real or tangible at stake, certainly not the stakes of a war.
He dropped out after eight months. He spent his mornings
in bed. In the afternoons he played pickup basketball at the

Y, and then at night he drove around town in his father's car, mostly alone, or with a six-pack of beer, cruising.

"The thing is," he wrote, "there's no place to go. Not just in this lousy little town. In general. My life, I mean. It's almost like I got killed over in Nam . . . Hard to describe. That night when Kiowa got wasted, I sort of sank down into the sewage with him . . . Feels like I'm still in deep shit."

The letter covered seventeen handwritten pages, its tone jumping from self-pity to anger to irony to guilt to a kind of feigned indifference. He didn't know what to feel. In the middle of the letter, for example, he reproached himself for complaining too much:

> God, this is starting to sound like some jerkoff vet crying in his beer. Sorry about that. I'm no basket case—not even any bad dreams. And I don't feel like anybody mistreats me or anything, except sometimes people act *too* nice, too polite, like they're afraid they might ask the wrong question . . . But I shouldn't bitch. One thing I hate—really hate—is all those whiner-vets. Guys sniveling about how they didn't get any parades. Such absolute crap. I mean, who in his right mind wants a *parade?* Or getting his back clapped by a bunch of patriotic idiots who don't know jack about what it feels like to kill people or get shot at or sleep in the rain or watch your buddy go down underneath the mud? Who *needs* it?
>
> Anyhow, I'm basically A-Okay. Home free!! So why not come down for a visit sometime and we'll chase pussy and shoot the breeze and tell each other old war lies? A good long bull session, you know?

I felt it coming, and near the end of the letter it came. He explained that he had read my first book, *If I Die in a*

*Combat Zone*, which he liked except for the "bleeding-heart political parts." For half a page he talked about how much the book had meant to him, how it brought back all kinds of memories, the villes and paddies and rivers, and how he recognized most of the characters, including himself, even though almost all of the names were changed. Then Bowker came straight out with it:

> What you should do, Tim, is write a story about a guy who feels like he got zapped over in that shithole. A guy who can't get his act together and just drives around town all day and can't think of any damn place to go and doesn't know how to get there anyway. This guy wants to talk about it, but he *can't* . . . If you want, you can use the stuff in this letter. (But not my real name, okay?) I'd write it myself except I can't ever find any words, if you know what I mean, and I can't figure out what exactly to *say*. Something about the field that night. The way Kiowa just disappeared into the crud. You were there—you can tell it.

Norman Bowker's letter hit me hard. For years I'd felt a certain smugness about how easily I had made the shift from war to peace. A nice smooth glide—no flashbacks or midnight sweats. The war was over, after all. And the thing to do was go on. So I took pride in sliding gracefully from Vietnam to graduate school, from Quang Ngai to Harvard, from one world to another. In ordinary conversation I never spoke much about the war, certainly not in detail, and yet ever since my return I had been talking about it virtually nonstop through my writing. Telling stories seemed a natural, inevitable process, like clearing the throat. Partly catharsis, partly communication, it was a way of grabbing people by the shirt and explaining exactly what had happened to me, how I'd allowed myself to get dragged into a wrong war, all the mistakes I'd made, all the terrible things I had seen and done.

I did not look on my work as therapy, and still don't. Yet when I received Norman Bowker's letter, it occurred to me that the act of writing had led me through a swirl of memories that might otherwise have ended in paralysis or worse. By telling stories, you objectify your own experience. You separate it from yourself. You pin down certain truths. You make up others. You start sometimes with an incident that truly happened, like the night in the shit field, and you carry it forward by inventing incidents that did not in fact occur but that nonetheless help to clarify and explain.

In any case, Norman Bowker's letter had an effect. It haunted me for more than a month, not the words so much as its desperation, and I resolved finally to take him up on his story suggestion. At the time I was at work on a new novel, *Going After Cacciato,* and one morning I sat down and began a chapter titled "Speaking of Courage." The emotional core came directly from Bowker's letter: the simple need to talk. To provide a dramatic frame, I collapsed events into a single time and place, a car circling a lake on a quiet afternoon in midsummer, using the lake as a nucleus around which the story would orbit. As he'd requested, I did not use Norman Bowker's name, instead substituting the name of my novel's main character, Paul Berlin. For the scenery I borrowed heavily from my own hometown. Wholesale thievery, in fact. I lifted up Worthington, Minnesota—the lake, the road, the causeway, the woman in pedal pushers, the junior college, the handsome houses and docks and boats and public parks—and carried it all a few hundred miles south and transplanted it onto the Iowa prairie.

The writing went quickly and easily. I drafted the piece in a week or two, fiddled with it for another week, then published it as a separate short story.

Almost immediately, though, there was a sense of failure. The details of Norman Bowker's story were missing. In this original version, which I still conceived as part of the novel, I had been forced to omit the shit field and the rain and the death of Kiowa, replacing this material with events that better fit the book's narrative. As a consequence I'd lost the natural counterpoint between the lake and the field. A metaphoric unity was broken. What the piece needed, and did not have, was the terrible killing power of that shit field.

As the novel developed over the next year, and as my own ideas clarified, it became apparent that the chapter had no proper home in the larger narrative. *Going After Cacciato* was a war story; "Speaking of Courage" was a postwar story. Two different time periods, two different sets of issues. There was no choice but to remove the chapter entirely. The mistake, in part, had been in trying to wedge the piece into a novel. Beyond that, though, something about the story had frightened me—I was afraid to speak directly, afraid to remember—and in the end the piece had been ruined by a failure to tell the full and precise truth about our night in the shit field.

Over the next several months, as it often happens, I managed to erase the story's flaws from my memory, taking pride in a shadowy, idealized recollection of its virtues. When the piece appeared in an anthology of short fiction, I sent a copy off to Norman Bowker with the thought that it might please him. His reaction was short and somewhat bitter.

"It's not terrible," he wrote me, "but you left out Vietnam. Where's Kiowa? Where's the shit?"

Eight months later he hanged himself.

In August of 1978 his mother sent me a brief note explaining what had happened. He'd been playing pickup basketball at the Y; after two hours he went off for a drink of water; he used a jump rope; his friends found him hanging from a water pipe. There was no suicide note, no message of any kind. "Norman was a quiet boy," his mother wrote, "and I don't suppose he wanted to bother anybody."

Now, a decade after his death, I'm hoping that "Speaking of Courage" makes good on Norman Bowker's silence. And I hope it's a better story. Although the old structure remains, the piece has been substantially revised, in some places by severe cutting, in other places by the addition of new material. Norman is back in the story, where he belongs, and I don't think he would mind that his real name appears. The central incident—our long night in the shit field along the Song Tra Bong—has been restored to the piece. It was hard stuff to write. Kiowa, after all, had been a close friend, and for years I've avoided thinking about his death and my own complicity in it. Even here it's not easy. In the interests of truth, however, I want to make it clear that Norman Bowker was in no way responsible for what happened to Kiowa. Norman did not experience a failure of nerve that night. He did not freeze up or lose the Silver Star for valor. That part of the story is my own.

# In the Field

At daybreak the platoon of eighteen soldiers formed into a loose rank and began tramping side by side through the deep muck of the shit field. They moved slowly in the rain. Leaning forward, heads down, they used the butts of their weapons as probes, wading across the field to the river and then turning and wading back again. They were tired and miserable; all they wanted now was to get it finished. Kiowa was gone. He was under the mud and water, folded in with the war, and their only thought was to find him and dig him out and then move on to some-place dry and warm. It had been a hard night. Maybe the worst ever. The rains had fallen without stop, and the Song Tra Bong had overflowed its banks, and the muck had now risen thigh-deep in the field along the river. A low, gray mist hovered over the land. Off to the west there was thunder, soft little moaning sounds, and the monsoons seemed to be a lasting element of the war. The eighteen soldiers moved in silence. First Lieutenant Jimmy Cross went first, now and then straightening out the rank, closing up the gaps. His uniform was dark with mud; his arms and face were filthy. Early in the morning he had radioed in the MIA report, giving the name and circumstances, but he was now determined to find his man, no matter what, even if it meant flying in slabs of concrete and damming up the river and draining the entire field. He would not lose a member of his command like this. It wasn't right. Kiowa had been a fine soldier and a fine human being, a devout Baptist, and there was no way Lieutenant Cross would allow such a good man to be lost under the slime of a shit field.

Briefly, he stopped and watched the clouds. Except for some occasional thunder it was a deeply quiet morning, just the rain and the steady sloshing sounds of eighteen men wading through the thick waters. Lieutenant Cross wished the rain would let up. Even for an hour, it would make things easier.

But then he shrugged. The rain was the war and you had to fight it.

Turning, he looked out across the field and yelled at one of his men to close up the rank. Not a man, really—a boy. The young soldier stood off by himself at the center of the field in knee-deep water, reaching down with both hands as if chasing some object just beneath the surface. The boy's shoulders were shaking. Jimmy Cross yelled again but the young soldier did not turn or look up. In his hooded poncho, everything caked with mud, the boy's face was impossible to make out. The filth seemed to erase identities, transforming the men into identical copies of a single soldier, which was exactly how Jimmy Cross had been trained to treat them, as interchangeable units of command. It was difficult sometimes, but he tried to avoid that sort of thinking. He had no military ambitions. He preferred to view his men not as units but as human beings. And Kiowa had been a splendid human being, the very best, intelligent and gentle and quiet-spoken. Very brave, too. And decent. The kid's father taught Sunday school in Oklahoma City, where Kiowa had been raised to believe in the promise of salvation under Jesus Christ, and this conviction had always been present in the boy's smile, in his posture toward the world, in the way he never went anywhere without an illustrated New Testament that his father had mailed to him as a birthday present back in January.

A crime, Jimmy Cross thought.

Looking out toward the river, he knew for a fact that he had made a mistake setting up here. The order had come from higher, true, but still he should've exercised some field discretion. He should've moved to higher ground for the night, should've radioed in false coordinates. There was nothing he could do now, but still it was a mistake and a hideous waste. He felt sick about it. Standing in the deep waters of the field, First Lieutenant Jimmy Cross began composing a letter in his head to the kid's father, not mentioning the shit field, just saying what a fine soldier Kiowa had been, what a fine human being, and how he was the kind of son that any father could be proud of forever.

The search went slowly. For a time the morning seemed to brighten, the sky going to a lighter shade of silver, but then the rains came back hard and steady. There was the feel of permanent twilight.

At the far left of the line, Azar and Norman Bowker and

Mitchell Sanders waded along the edge of the field closest to the river. They were tall men, but at times the muck came to midthigh, other times to the crotch.

Azar kept shaking his head. He coughed and shook his head and said, "Man, talk about irony. I bet if Kiowa was here, I bet he'd just laugh. Eating shit—it's your classic irony."

"Fine," said Norman Bowker. "Now pipe down."

Azar sighed. "Wasted in the waste," he said. "A shit field. You got to admit, it's pure world-class irony."

The three men moved with slow, heavy steps. It was hard to keep balance. Their boots sank into the ooze, which produced a powerful downward suction, and with each step they would have to pull up hard to break the hold. The rain made quick dents in the water, like tiny mouths, and the stink was everywhere.

When they reached the river, they shifted a few meters to the north and began wading back up the field. Occasionally they used their weapons to test the bottom, but mostly they just searched with their feet.

"A classic case," Azar was saying. "Biting the dirt, so to speak, that tells the story."

"Enough," Bowker said.

"Like those old cowboy movies. One more redskin bites the dirt."

"I'm serious, man. Zip it shut."

Azar smiled and said, "Classic."

The morning was cold and wet. They had not slept during the night, not even for a few moments, and all three of them were feeling the tension as they moved across the field toward the river. There was nothing they could do for Kiowa.

Just find him and slide him aboard a chopper. Whenever a man died it was always the same, a desire to get it over with quickly, no frills or ceremony, and what they wanted now was to head for a ville and get under a roof and forget what had happened during the night.

Halfway across the field Mitchell Sanders stopped. He stood for a moment with his eyes shut, feeling along the bottom with a foot, then he passed his weapon over to Norman Bowker and reached down into the muck. After a second he hauled up a scummy green rucksack.

The three men did not speak for a time. The pack was heavy with mud and water, dead-looking. Inside were a pair of moccasins and an illustrated New Testament.

"Well," Mitchell Sanders finally said, "the guy's around here somewhere."

"Better tell the LT."

"Screw him."

"Yeah, but—"

"Some lieutenant," Sanders said. "Camps us in a toilet. Man don't *know* shit."

"Nobody knew," Bowker said.

"Maybe so, maybe not. Ten billion places we could've set up last night, the man picks a latrine."

Norman Bowker stared down at the rucksack. It was made of dark green nylon with an aluminum frame, but now it had the curious look of flesh.

"It wasn't the LT's fault," Bowker said quietly.

"Whose then?"

"Nobody's. Nobody knew till afterward."

Mitchell Sanders made a sound in his throat. He hoisted up the rucksack, slipped into the harness, and pulled the straps tight. "All right, but this much for sure. The man knew it was raining. He knew about the river. One plus one. Add it up, you get exactly what happened." Sanders glared at the river. "Move it," he said. "Kiowa's waiting on us." Slowly then, bending against the rain, Azar and Norman Bowker and Mitchell Sanders began wading again through the deep waters, their eyes down, circling out from where they had found the rucksack.

First Lieutenant Jimmy Cross stood fifty meters away. He had finished writing the letter in his head, explaining things to Kiowa's father, and now he folded his arms and watched his platoon crisscrossing the wide field. In a funny way, it reminded him of the municipal golf course in his hometown in New Jersey. A lost ball, he thought. Tired players searching through the rough, sweeping back and forth in long systematic patterns. He wished he were there right now. On the sixth hole. Looking out across the water hazard that fronted the small flat green, a seven iron in his hand, calculating wind and distance, wondering if he should reach instead for an eight. A tough decision, but all you could ever lose was a ball. You did not lose a player. And you never had to wade out into the hazard and spend the day searching through the slime.

Jimmy Cross did not want the responsibility of leading these men. He had never wanted it. In his sophomore year at Mount Sebastian College he had signed up for the Reserve Officer Training Corps without much thought. An automatic thing: because his friends had joined, and because it was worth a few credits, and because it seemed preferable to letting the draft take him. He was unprepared. Twenty-four years old and his heart wasn't in it. Military matters meant nothing to him. He did not care one way or the other about the war, and he had no desire to command, and even after all these months in the bush, all the days and nights, even then he did not know enough to keep his men out of a shit field.

What he should've done, he told himself, was follow his first impulse. In the late afternoon yesterday, when they reached the night coordinates, he should've taken one look and headed for higher ground. No excuses. At one edge of the field was a small ville, and right away a couple of old mama-sans had trotted out to warn him. Number ten, they'd said. Evil ground. But it was a war, and he had his orders, so they'd set up a perimeter and crawled under their ponchos and tried to settle in for the night. He remembered how the water kept rising, how a terrible stink began to swell up out of the earth. It was a dead-fish smell, partly, but something else, too, and then late in the night Mitchell Sanders had crawled through the rain and grabbed him hard by the arm and asked what he was doing setting up in a shit field. The village toilet, Sanders said. He remembered the look on Sanders's face. The guy stared for a moment and then wiped his mouth and whispered, "Shit," and then crawled away into the dark.

A stupid mistake. That's all it was, a mistake, but it had killed Kiowa.

Lieutenant Jimmy Cross felt something tighten inside him. In the letter to Kiowa's father he would apologize point-blank. Just admit to the blunders.

He would place the blame where it belonged. Tactically, he'd say, it was indefensible ground from the start. Low and flat. No natural cover. And so late in the night, when they took mortar fire from across the river, all they could do was snake down under the slop and lie there and wait. The field just exploded. Rain and slop and shrapnel, it all mixed together, and the field seemed to boil. He would explain this to Kiowa's father. Carefully, not covering up his own guilt, he would tell how the mortar rounds made craters in the slush, spraying up great showers of filth, and how the craters then collapsed on themselves and filled up with mud and water, sucking things down, swallowing things, weapons and entrenching tools and belts of ammunition, and how in this way his son Kiowa had been combined with the waste and the war.

My own fault, he would say.

Straightening up, First Lieutenant Jimmy Cross rubbed his eyes and tried to get his thoughts together. The rain fell in a cold, sad drizzle.

Off toward the river he again noticed the young soldier standing alone at the center of the field. The boy's shoulders were shaking. Maybe it was something in the posture of the soldier, or the way he seemed to be reaching for some invisible object beneath the surface, but for several moments Jimmy Cross stood very still, afraid to move, yet knowing he had to, and then he murmured to himself, "My fault," and he nodded and waded out across the field toward the boy.

The young soldier was trying hard not to cry.

He, too, blamed himself. Bent forward at the waist, groping with both hands, he seemed to be chasing some creature just beyond reach, something elusive, a fish or a frog. His lips were moving. Like Jimmy Cross, the boy was explaining things to an absent judge. It wasn't to defend himself. The boy recognized his own guilt and wanted only to lay out the full causes.

Wading sideways a few steps, he leaned down and felt along the soft bottom of the field.

He pictured Kiowa's face. They'd been close buddies, the tightest, and he remembered how last night they had huddled together under their ponchos, the rain cold and steady, the water rising to their knees, but how Kiowa had just laughed it off and said they should concentrate on better things. And so for a long while they'd talked about their families and hometowns. At one point, the boy remembered, he'd been showing Kiowa a picture of his girlfriend. He remembered switching on his flashlight. A stupid thing to do, but he did it anyway, and he remembered Kiowa leaning in for a look at the picture— "Hey, she's *cute*," he'd said—and then the field exploded all around them.

Like murder, the boy thought. The flashlight made it happen. Dumb and dangerous. And as a result his friend Kiowa was dead.

That simple, he thought.

He wished there were some other way to look at it, but there wasn't. Very simple and very final. He remembered two mortar rounds hitting close by. Then a third, even closer, and off to his left he'd heard somebody scream. The voice was ragged and clotted up, but he knew instantly that it was Kiowa.

He remembered trying to crawl toward the screaming. No sense of direction, though, and the field seemed to suck him under, and everything was black and wet, and he couldn't get his bearings, and then another round hit nearby, and for a few moments all he could do was hold his breath and duck down beneath the water.

Later, when he came up again, there were no more screams. There was an arm and a wristwatch and part of a boot. There were bubbles where Kiowa's head should've been.

He remembered grabbing the boot. He remembered pulling hard, but how the field seemed to pull back, like a tug-of-war he couldn't win, and how finally he had to whisper his friend's name and let go and watch the boot slide away. Then for a long time there were things he could not remember. Various sounds, various smells. Later he'd found himself lying on a little rise, face-up, tasting the field in his mouth, listening to the rain and explosions and bubbling sounds. He was alone. He'd lost everything. He'd lost Kiowa and his weapon and his flashlight and his girlfriend's picture. He remembered this. He remembered wondering if he could lose himself.

Now, in the dull morning rain, the boy seemed frantic. He waded quickly from spot to spot, leaning down and plunging his hands into the water. He did not look up when Lieutenant Jimmy Cross approached.

"Right here," the boy was saying. "Got to be right here."

Jimmy Cross remembered the kid's face but not the name. That happened sometimes. He tried to treat his men as individuals but sometimes the names just escaped him.

He watched the young soldier shove his hands into the water. "Right *here*," he kept saying. His movements seemed random and jerky.

Jimmy Cross waited a moment, then stepped closer. "Listen," he said quietly, "the guy could be anywhere."

The boy glanced up. "Who could?"

"Kiowa. You can't expect—"

"Kiowa's *dead*."

"Well, yes."

The young soldier nodded. "So what about Billie?"

"Who?"

"My girl. What about her? This picture, it was the only one I had. Right here, I lost it."

Jimmy Cross shook his head. It bothered him that he could not come up with a name.

"Slow down," he said, "I don't—"

"Billie's *picture*. I had it all wrapped up, I had it in plastic, so it'll be okay if I can . . . Last night we were looking at it, me and Kiowa. Right here. I know for sure it's right here somewhere."

Jimmy Cross smiled at the boy. "You can ask her for another one. A better one."

"She won't *send* another one. She's not even my *girl* anymore, she won't . . . Man, I got to find it."

The boy yanked his arm free.

He shuffled sideways and stooped down again and dipped into the muck with both hands. His shoulders were shaking. Briefly, Lieutenant Cross wondered where the kid's weapon was, and his helmet, but it seemed better not to ask.

He felt some pity come on him. For a moment the day seemed to soften. So much hurt, he thought. He watched the young soldier wading through the water, bending down and then standing and then bending down again, as if something might finally be salvaged from all the waste.

Jimmy Cross silently wished the boy luck.

Then he closed his eyes and went back to working on the letter to Kiowa's father.

. . .

Across the field Azar and Norman Bowker and Mitchell Sanders were wading alongside a narrow dike at the edge of the field. It was near noon now.

Norman Bowker found Kiowa. He was under two feet of water. Nothing showed except the heel of a boot.

"That's him?" Azar said.

"Who else?"

"I don't know." Azar shook his head. "I don't know."

Norman Bowker touched the boot, covered his eyes for a moment, then stood up and looked at Azar.

"So where's the joke?" he said.

"No joke."

"Eating shit. Let's hear that one."

"Forget it."

Mitchell Sanders told them to knock it off. The three soldiers moved to the dike, put down their packs and weapons, then waded back to where the boot was showing. The body lay partly wedged under a layer of mud beneath the water. It was hard to get traction; with each movement the muck would grip their feet and hold tight. The rain had come back harder now. Mitchell Sanders reached down and found Kiowa's other boot, and they waited a moment, then Sanders sighed and said, "Okay," and they took hold of the two boots and pulled up hard. There was only a slight give. They tried again, but this time the body did not move at all. After the third try they stopped and looked down for a while. "One more time," Norman Bowker said. He counted to three and they leaned back and pulled.

"Stuck," said Mitchell Sanders.

"I see that. Christ."

They tried again, then called over Henry Dobbins and

Rat Kiley, and all five of them put their arms and backs into it, but the body was jammed in tight.

Azar moved to the dike and sat holding his stomach. His face was pale.

The others stood in a circle, watching the water, then after a time somebody said, "We can't just *leave* him there," and the men nodded and got out their entrenching tools and began digging. It was hard, sloppy work. The mud seemed to flow back faster than they could dig, but Kiowa was their friend and they kept at it anyway.

Slowly, in little groups, the rest of the platoon drifted over to watch. Only Lieutenant Jimmy Cross and the young soldier were still searching the field.

"What we should do, I guess," Norman Bowker said, "is tell the LT."

Mitchell Sanders shook his head. "Just mess things up. Besides, the man looks happy out there, real content. Let him be."

After ten minutes they uncovered most of Kiowa's lower body. The corpse was angled steeply into the muck, upside down, like a diver who had plunged headfirst off a high tower. The men stood quietly for a few seconds. There was a feeling of awe. Mitchell Sanders finally nodded and said, "Let's get it done," and they took hold of the legs and pulled up hard, then pulled again, and after a moment Kiowa came sliding to the surface. A piece of his shoulder was missing; the arms and chest and face were cut up with shrapnel. He was covered with bluish green mud. "Well," Henry Dobbins said, "it could be worse," and Dave Jensen said, "How, man? Tell me *how*." Carefully, trying not to look at the body, they carried Kiowa over to the dike and laid him down. They used towels to clean off the scum. Rat Kiley went through the kid's pockets, placed his personal effects in a plastic bag, taped the bag to Kiowa's wrist, then used the radio to call in a dustoff.

Moving away, the men found things to do with themselves, some smoking, some opening up cans of C rations, a few just standing in the rain.

For all of them it was a relief to have it finished. There was the promise now of finding a hootch somewhere, or an abandoned pagoda, where they could strip down and wring out their fatigues and maybe start a hot fire. They felt bad for Kiowa. But they also felt a kind of giddiness, a secret joy, because they were alive, and because even the rain was preferable to being sucked under a shit field, and because it was all a matter of luck and happenstance.

Azar sat down on the dike next to Norman Bowker.

"Listen," he said. "Those dumb jokes—I didn't mean anything."

"We all say things."

"Yeah, but when I saw the guy, it made me feel—I don't know—like he was listening."

"He wasn't."

"I guess not. But I felt sort of guilty almost, like if I'd kept my mouth shut none of it would've ever happened. Like it was my fault."

Norman Bowker looked out across the wet field.

"Nobody's fault," he said. "Everybody's."

Near the center of the field First Lieutenant Jimmy Cross squatted in the muck, almost entirely submerged. In his head he was revising the letter to Kiowa's father. Impersonal this time. An officer expressing an officer's condolences. No apologies were necessary, because in fact it was one of those freak things, and the war was full of freaks, and nothing could ever change it anyway. Which was the truth, he thought. The exact truth.

Lieutenant Cross went deeper into the muck, the dark water at his throat, and tried to tell himself it was the truth.

Beside him, a few steps off to the left, the young soldier was still searching for his girlfriend's picture. Still remembering how he had killed Kiowa.

The boy wanted to confess. He wanted to tell the lieutenant how in the middle of the night he had pulled out Billie's picture and passed it over to Kiowa and then switched on the flashlight, and how Kiowa had whispered, "Hey, she's *cute*," and how for a second the flashlight had made Billie's face sparkle, and how right then the field had exploded all around them. The flashlight had done it. Like a target shining in the dark.

The boy looked up at the sky, then at Jimmy Cross.

"Sir?" he said.

The rain and mist moved across the field in broad, sweeping sheets of gray. Close by, there was thunder.

"Sir," the boy said, "I got to explain something."

But Lieutenant Jimmy Cross wasn't listening. Eyes closed, he let himself go deeper into the waste, just letting the field take him. He lay back and floated.

When a man died, there had to be blame. Jimmy Cross understood this. You could blame the war. You could blame the idiots who made the war. You could blame Kiowa for going to it. You could blame the rain. You could blame the river. You could blame the field, the mud, the climate.

You could blame the enemy. You could blame the mortar rounds. You could blame people who were too lazy to read a newspaper, who were bored by the daily body counts, who switched channels at the mention of politics. You could blame whole nations. You could blame God. You could blame the munitions makers or Karl Marx or a trick of fate or an old man in Omaha who forgot to vote.

In the field, though, the causes were immediate. A moment of carelessness or bad judgment or plain stupidity carried consequences that lasted forever.

For a long while Jimmy Cross lay floating. In the clouds to the east there was the sound of a helicopter, but he did not take notice. With his eyes still closed, bobbing in the field, he let himself slip away. He was back home in New Jersey. A golden afternoon on the golf course, the fairways lush and green, and he was teeing it up on the first hole. It was a world without responsibility. When the war was over, he thought, maybe then he would write a letter to Kiowa's father. Or maybe not. Maybe he would just take a couple of practice swings and knock the ball down the middle and pick up his clubs and walk off into the afternoon.

# Good Form

It's time to be blunt. I'm forty-three years old, true, and I'm a writer now, and a long time ago I walked through Quang Ngai Province as a foot soldier.

Almost everything else is invented.

But it's not a game. It's a form. Right here, now, as I invent myself, I'm thinking of all I want to tell you about why this book is written as it is. For instance, I want to tell you this: twenty years ago I watched a man die on a trail near the village of My Khe. I did not kill him. But I was present, you see, and my presence was guilt enough. I remember his face, which was not a pretty face, because his jaw was in his throat, and I remember feeling the burden of responsibility and grief. I blamed myself. And rightly so, because I was present.

But listen. Even *that* story is made up.

I want you to feel what I felt. I want you to know why story-truth is truer sometimes than happening-truth.

Here is the happening-truth. I was once a soldier. There

were many bodies, real bodies with real faces, but I was young then and I was afraid to look. And now, twenty years later, I'm left with faceless responsibility and faceless grief.

Here is the story-truth. He was a slim, dead, almost dainty young man of about twenty. He lay in the center of a red clay trail near the village of My Khe. His jaw was in his throat. His one eye was shut, the other eye was a star-shaped hole. I killed him.

What stories can do, I guess, is make things present.

I can look at things I never looked at. I can attach faces to grief and love and pity and God. I can be brave. I can make myself feel again.

"Daddy, tell the truth," Kathleen can say, "did you ever kill anybody?" And I can say, honestly, "Of course not."

Or I can say, honestly, "Yes."

# Field Trip

A few months after completing "In the Field," I returned with my daughter to Vietnam, where we visited the site of Kiowa's death, and where I looked for signs of forgiveness or personal grace or whatever else the land might offer. The field was still there, though not as I remembered it. Much smaller, I thought, and not nearly so menacing, and in the bright sunlight it was hard to picture what had happened on this ground some twenty years ago. Except for a few marshy spots along the river, everything was bone dry. No ghosts—just a flat, grassy field. The place was at peace. There were yellow butterflies. There was a breeze and a wide blue sky. Along the river two old farmers stood in ankle-deep water, repairing the same narrow dike where we had laid out Kiowa's body after pulling him from the muck. Things were quiet. At one point, I remember, one of the farmers looked up and shaded his eyes, staring across the field at us, then after a time he wiped his forehead and went back to work.

I stood with my arms folded, feeling the grip of sentiment and time. Amazing, I thought. Twenty years.

Behind me, in the jeep, my daughter Kathleen sat waiting with a government interpreter, and now and then I could hear the two of them talking in soft voices. They were already fast friends. Neither of them, I think, understood what all this was about, why I'd insisted that we search out this spot. It had been a hard two-hour ride from Quang Ngai City, bumpy dirt roads and a hot August sun, ending up at an empty field on the edge of nowhere.

I took out my camera, snapped a couple of pictures, and stood gazing out at the field. After a time Kathleen got out of the jeep and stood beside me.

"You know what I think?" she said. "I think this place stinks. It smells like ... God, I don't even *know* what. It smells rotten."

"It sure does. I know that."

"So when can we go?"

"Pretty soon," I said.

She started to say something but then hesitated. Frowning, she squinted out at the field for a second, then shrugged and walked back to the jeep.

Kathleen had just turned ten, and this trip was a kind of birthday present, showing her the world, offering a small piece of her father's history. For the most part she'd held up well—far better than I—and over the first two weeks she'd trooped along without complaint as we hit the obligatory tourist stops. Ho Chi Minh's mausoleum in Hanoi. A model farm outside Saigon. The tunnels at Cu Chi. The monuments and government offices and orphanages. Through most of this, Kathleen had seemed to enjoy the foreignness of it all, the exotic food and animals, and even during those periods of boredom and discomfort she'd kept up a good-humored tolerance. At the same time, however, she'd seemed a bit puzzled. The war was as remote to her as cavemen and dinosaurs.

One morning in Saigon she'd asked what it was all about. "This whole war," she said, "why was everybody so mad at everybody else?"

I shook my head. "They weren't mad, exactly. Some people wanted one thing, other people wanted another thing."

"What did *you* want?"

"Nothing," I said. "To stay alive."

"That's all?"

"Yes."

Kathleen sighed. "Well, I don't get it. I mean, how come you were even here in the first place?"

"I don't know," I said. "Because I had to be."

"But *why?*"

I tried to find something to tell her, but finally I shrugged and said, "It's a mystery, I guess. I don't know."

For the rest of the day she was very quiet. That night, though, just before bedtime, Kathleen put her hand on my shoulder and said, "You know something? Sometimes you're pretty weird, aren't you?"

"Well, no," I said.

"You are *too.*" She pulled her hand away and frowned at me. "Like coming over here. Some dumb thing happens a long time ago and you can't ever forget it."

"And that's bad?"

"No," she said. "That's weird."

In the second week of August, near the end of our stay, I'd arranged for the side trip up to Quang Ngai. The tourist stuff was fine, but from the start I'd wanted to take my daughter to the places I'd seen as a soldier. I wanted to show her the Vietnam that kept me awake at night—a shady trail outside the village of My Khe, a filthy old pigsty on the Batangan Peninsula. Our time was short, however, and choices had to be made, and in the end I decided to take her to this piece of ground where my friend Kiowa had died. It seemed appropriate. And, besides, I had business here.

Now, looking out at the field, I wondered if it was all a mistake. Everything was too ordinary. A quiet sunny day, and the field was not the field I remembered. I pictured Kiowa's face, the way he used to smile, but all I felt was the awkwardness of remembering.

Behind me, Kathleen let out a little giggle. The interpreter was showing her magic tricks.

There were birds and butterflies, the soft rustlings of rural-anywhere. Below, in the earth, the relics of our presence were no doubt still there, the canteens and bandoliers and mess kits. This little field, I thought, had swallowed so much. My best friend. My pride. My belief in myself as a man of some small dignity and courage. Still, it was hard to find any real emotion. It simply wasn't there. After that long night in the rain, I'd seemed to grow cold inside, all the illusions gone, all the old ambitions and hopes for myself sucked away into the mud. Over the years, that coldness had never entirely disappeared. There were times in my life when I couldn't feel much, not sadness or pity or passion, and somehow I blamed this place for what I had become, and I blamed it for taking away the person I had once been. For twenty years this field had embodied all the waste that was Vietnam, all the vulgarity and horror.

Now, it was just what it was. Flat and dreary and unremarkable. I walked up toward the river, trying to pick out specific landmarks, but all I recognized was a small rise where Jimmy Cross had set up his command post that night. Nothing else. For a while I watched the two old farmers working under the hot sun. I took a few more photographs, waved at the farmers, then turned and moved back to the jeep.

Kathleen gave me a little nod.

"Well," she said, "I hope you're having fun."

"Sure."

"Can we go now?

"In a minute," I said. "Just relax."

At the back of the jeep I found the small cloth bundle I'd carried over from the States.

Kathleen's eyes narrowed. "What's *that?*"

"Stuff," I told her.

She glanced at the bundle again, then hopped out of the jeep and followed me back to the field. We walked past Jimmy Cross's command post, past the spot where Kiowa had gone under, down to where the field dipped into the marshland along the river. I took off my shoes and socks.

"Okay," Kathleen said, "what's going on?"

"A quick swim."

"Where?"

"Right here," I said. "Stay put."

She watched me unwrap the cloth bundle. Inside were Kiowa's old moccasins.

I stripped down to my underwear, took off my wristwatch, and waded in. The water was warm against my feet. Instantly, I recognized the soft, fat feel of the bottom. The water here was eight inches deep.

Kathleen seemed nervous. She squinted at me, her hands fluttering. "Listen, this is stupid," she said, "you can't even hardly get wet. How can you *swim* out there?"

"I'll manage."

"But it's not . . . I mean, God, it's not even water, it's like mush or something."

She pinched her nose and watched me wade out to where the water reached my knees. Roughly here, I decided, was where Mitchell Sanders had found Kiowa's rucksack. I eased myself down, squatting at first, then sitting. There was again that sense of recognition. The water rose to mid-chest, a deep greenish brown, almost hot. Small water bugs skipped along the surface. Right here, I thought. Leaning forward, I reached in with the moccasins and wedged them into the soft bottom, letting them slide away. Tiny bubbles broke along the surface. I tried to think of something decent to say, something meaningful and right, but nothing came to me.

I looked down into the field.

"Well," I finally managed. "There it is."

My voice surprised me. It had a rough, chalky sound, full of things I did not know were there. I wanted to tell Kiowa that he'd been a great friend, the very best, but all I could do was slap hands with the water.

The sun made me squint. Twenty years. A lot like yesterday, a lot like never. In a way, maybe, I'd gone under with Kiowa, and now after two decades I'd mostly worked my way out. A hot afternoon, a bright August sun, and the war was over. For a few moments I could not bring myself to move. Like waking from a summer nap, feeling lazy and sluggish, the world collecting itself around me. Fifty meters up the field one of the old farmers stood watching from along the dike. The man's face was dark and solemn. As we stared at each other, neither of us moving, I felt something go shut in my heart while something else swung open. For a second, I wondered if the old man might walk over to exchange a few war stories, but instead he picked up a shovel and raised it over his head and held it there for a time, grimly, like a flag, then he brought the shovel down and said something to his friend and began digging into the hard, dry ground.

I stood up and waded out of the water.

"What a mess," Kathleen said. "All that gunk on your skin, you look like . . . Wait'll I tell Mommy, she'll probably make you sleep in the garage."

"You're right," I said. "Don't tell her."

I pulled on my shoes, took my daughter's hand, and led her across the field toward the jeep. Soft heat waves shimmied up out of the earth.

When we reached the jeep, Kathleen turned and glanced out at the field.

"That old man," she said, "is he mad at you or something?"

"I hope not."

"He *looks* mad."

"No," I said. "All that's finished."

# The Ghost Soldiers

I was shot twice. The first time, out by Tri Binh, it knocked me against the pagoda wall, and I bounced and spun around and ended up on Rat Kiley's lap. A lucky thing, because Rat was the medic. He tied on a compress and told me to ease back, then he ran off toward the fighting. For a long time I lay there all alone, listening to the battle, thinking *I've been shot, I've been shot:* all those Gene Autry movies I'd seen as a kid. In fact, I almost smiled, except then I started to think I might die. It was the fear, mostly, but I felt wobbly, and then I had a sinking sensation, ears all plugged up, as if I'd gone deep under water. Thank God for Rat Kiley. Every so often, maybe four times altogether, he trotted back to check me out. Which took courage. It was a wild fight, guys running and laying down fire and regrouping and running again, lots of noise, but Rat Kiley took the risks. "Easy does it," he told me, "just a side wound, no problem unless you're pregnant." He ripped off the compress, applied a fresh one, and told me to clamp it in place with my fingers.

"Press hard," he said. "Don't worry about the baby." Then he took off. It was almost dark when the fighting ended and the chopper came to take me and two dead guys away. "Happy trails," Rat said. He helped me into the helicopter and stood there for a moment. Then he did an odd thing. He leaned in and put his head against my shoulder and almost hugged me. Coming from Rat Kiley, that was something new.

On the ride into Chu Lai, I kept waiting for the pain to hit, but in fact I didn't feel much. A throb, that's all. Even in the hospital it wasn't bad.

When I got back to Alpha Company twenty-six days later, in mid-December, Rat Kiley had been wounded and shipped off to Japan, and a new medic named Bobby Jorgenson had replaced him. Jorgenson was no Rat Kiley. He was green and incompetent and scared. So when I got shot the second time, in the butt, along the Song Tra Bong, it took the son of a bitch almost ten minutes to work up the nerve to crawl over to me. By then I was gone with the pain. Later I found out I'd almost died of shock. Bobby Jorgenson didn't know about shock, or if he did, the fear made him forget. To make it worse, he bungled the patch job, and a couple of weeks later my ass started to rot away. You could actually peel off fillets of meat with your fingernail.

It was borderline gangrene. I spent a month flat on my stomach; I couldn't walk or sit; I couldn't sleep. I kept seeing Bobby Jorgenson's scared-white face. Those buggy eyes and the way his lips twitched and that silly excuse he had for a mustache. After the rot cleared up, once I could think straight, I devoted a lot of time to figuring ways to get back at him.

. . .

Getting shot should be an experience from which you can draw some small pride. I don't mean the macho stuff. All I mean is that you should be able to *talk* about it: the stiff thump of the bullet, like a fist, the way it knocks the air out of you and makes you cough, how the sound of the gunshot arrives about ten years later, and the dizzy feeling, the smell of yourself, the things you think about and say and do right afterward, the way your eyes focus on a tiny white pebble or a blade of grass and how you start thinking, Oh man, that's the last thing I'll ever see, *that* pebble, *that* blade of grass, which makes you want to cry.

Pride isn't the right word. I don't know the right word. All I know is, you shouldn't feel embarrassed. Humiliation shouldn't be part of it.

Diaper rash, the nurses called it. An in-joke, I suppose. But it made me hate Bobby Jorgenson the way some guys hated the VC, gut hate, the kind of hate that stays with you even in your dreams.

I guess the higher-ups decided I'd been shot enough. At the end of December, when I was released from the 91st Evac Hospital, they transferred me over to Headquarters Company—S-4, the battalion supply section. Compared with the boonies it was cushy duty. We had regular hours. There was an EM club with beer and movies, sometimes even live floor shows, the whole blurry slow motion of the rear. For the first time in months I felt reasonably safe. The battalion firebase was built into a hill just off Highway 1, surrounded on all sides by flat paddy land, and between us and the paddies there were reinforced bunkers and observation towers and trip flares and rolls of razor-tipped barbed wire.

You could still die, of course—once a month we'd get hit with mortar fire—but you could also die in the bleachers at Met Stadium in Minneapolis, bases loaded, Harmon Killebrew coming to the plate.

I didn't complain. In an odd way, though, there were times when I missed the adventure, even the danger, of the real war out in the boonies. It's a hard thing to explain to somebody who hasn't felt it, but the presence of death and danger has a way of bringing you fully awake. It makes things vivid. When you're afraid, really afraid, you see things you never saw before, you pay attention to the world. You make close friends. You become part of a tribe and you share the same blood—you give it together, you take it together. On the other hand, I'd already been hit with two bullets; I was superstitious; I believed in the odds with the same passion that my friend Kiowa had once believed in Jesus Christ, or the way Mitchell Sanders believed in the power of morals. I figured my war was over. If it hadn't been for the constant ache in my butt, I'm sure things would've worked out fine.

But it hurt.

At night I had to sleep on my belly. That doesn't sound so terrible until you consider that I'd been a back-sleeper all my life. I'd lie there all fidgety and tight, then after a while I'd feel a swell of anger come on. I'd squirm around, cussing, half nuts with pain, and pretty soon I'd start remembering how Bobby Jorgenson had almost killed me. Shock, I'd think—how could he forget to treat for shock? I'd remember how long it took him to get to me, and how his fingers were all jerky and nervous, and the way his lips kept twitching under that ridiculous little mustache.

The nights were miserable. Sometimes I'd roam around the base. I'd head down to the wire and stare out at the darkness, out where the war was, and think up ways to make Bobby Jorgenson feel exactly what I felt. I wanted to hurt him.

In March, Alpha Company came in for stand-down. I was there at the helipad to meet the choppers. Mitchell Sanders and Azar and Henry Dobbins and Dave Jensen and Norman Bowker slapped hands with me and we piled their gear in my jeep and drove down to the Alpha hootches. We partied until chow time. Afterward, we kept on partying. It was one of the rituals. Even if you weren't in the mood, you did it on principle.

By midnight it was story time.

"Morty Phillips used up his luck," Bowker said.

I smiled and waited. There was a tempo to how stories got told. Bowker peeled open a finger blister and sucked on it.

"Go on," Azar said. "Tell him everything."

"Well, that's about it. Poor Morty wasted his luck. Pissed it away."

"On nothing," Azar said. "The dummy pisses it away on *nothing.*"

Norman Bowker nodded, started to speak, but then stopped and got up and moved to the cooler and shoved his hands deep into the ice. He was naked except for his shorts and dog tags. In a way, I envied him—all of them. Their deep bush tans, the sores and blisters, the stories, the in-it-togetherness. I felt close to them, yes, but I also felt a new sense of separation. My fatigues were starched; I had a neat haircut and the clean, sterile smell of the rear. They were still my buddies, at least on one level, but once you leave the boonies, the whole comrade business gets turned around. You become a civilian. You forfeit membership in the family, the blood fraternity, and no matter how hard you try, you can't pretend to be part of it.

That's how I felt—like a civilian—and it made me sad. These guys had been my brothers. We'd loved one another.

Norman Bowker bent forward and scooped up some ice against his chest, pressing it there for a moment, then he fished out a beer and snapped it open.

"It was out by My Khe," he said quietly. "One of those killer hot days, hot-hot, and we're all popping salt tabs just to stay conscious. Can't barely breathe. Everybody's lying around, just grooving it, and after a while somebody says, 'Hey, where's Morty?' So the lieutenant does a head count, and guess what? No Morty."

"Gone," Azar said. "Poof. No fuckin' Morty."

Norman Bowker nodded. "Anyhow, we send out two search patrols. No dice. Not a trace." Pausing a second, Bowker poured a trickle of beer onto his blister and licked at it. "By then it's almost dark. Lieutenant Cross, he's ready to have a fit—you know how he gets, right?—and then, guess what? Take a guess."

"Morty shows," I said.

"You got it, man. Morty shows. We almost chalk him up as MIA, and then, bingo, he shows."

"Soaking wet," said Azar.

"Hey, listen—"

"Okay, but *tell* it."

Norman Bowker frowned. "Soaking wet," he said. "Turns

out the moron went for a swim. You *believe* that? All alone, he just takes off, hikes a couple klicks, finds himself a river and strips down and hops in and starts doing the goddamn breast stroke or some such fine shit. No security, no nothing. I mean, the dude goes skinny dipping."

Azar giggled. "A hot day."

"Not that hot," said Dave Jensen.

"Hot, though."

"Get the picture?" Bowker said. "This is My Khe we're talking about, dinks everywhere, and the guy goes for a *swim*."

"Crazy," I said.

I looked across the hootch. Twenty or thirty guys were there, some drinking, some passed out, but I couldn't find Morty Phillips among them.

Bowker smiled. He reached out and put his hand on my knee and squeezed.

"That's the kicker, man. No more Morty."

"No?"

"Morty's luck gets all used up," Bowker said. His hand still rested on my knee, very lightly. "A few days later, maybe a week, he feels real dizzy. Pukes a lot, temperature zooms way up. I mean, the guy's *sick*. Jorgenson says he must've swallowed bad water on that swim. Swallowed a VC virus or something."

"Bobby Jorgenson," I said. "Where is he?"

"Be cool."

"Where's my good buddy Bobby?"

Norman Bowker made a short clicking sound with his tongue. "You want to hear this? Yes or no?"

"Sure I do."

"So listen up, then. Morty gets sick. Like you never seen

nobody so bad off. This is real kickass disease, he can't walk or talk, can't fart. Can't nothin'. Like he's paralyzed. Polio, maybe."

Henry Dobbins shook his head. "Not polio. You got it wrong."

"*Maybe* polio."

"No way," said Dobbins. "Not polio."

"Well, hey," Bowker said, "I'm just saying what Jorgenson says. Maybe fuckin' polio. Or that weird elephant disease. Elephantiasshole or whatever."

"Yeah, but not polio."

Across the hootch, sitting off by himself, Azar grinned and snapped his fingers. "Either way," he said, "it goes to show you. Don't throw away luck on little stuff. Save it up."

"There it is," said Mitchell Sanders.

"Morty was due," Dave Jensen said.

"Overdue," Sanders said.

Norman Bowker nodded solemnly. "You don't mess around like that. You just don't fritter away all your luck."

"Amen," said Sanders.

"Fuckin' polio," said Henry Dobbins.

We sat quietly for a time. There was no need to talk, because we were thinking the same things: about Morty Phillips and the way luck worked and didn't work and how it was impossible to calculate the odds. There were a million ways to die. Getting shot was one way. Booby traps and land mines and gangrene and shock and polio from a VC virus.

"Where's Jorgenson?" I said.

Another thing. Three times a day, no matter what, I had to stop whatever I was doing. I had to go find a private place and drop my pants and smear on this antibacterial ointment.

The stuff left stains on the seat of my trousers, big yellow splotches, and so naturally there were some jokes. There was one about rear guard duty. There was another one about hemorrhoids and how I had trouble putting the past behind me. The others weren't quite so funny.

During the first full day of Alpha's stand-down, I didn't run into Bobby Jorgenson once. Not at chow, not at the EM club, not even during our long booze sessions in the Alpha Company hootch. At one point I almost went looking for him, but my friend Mitchell Sanders told me to forget it.

"Let it ride," he said. "The kid messed up bad, for sure, but you have to take into account how green he was. Brandnew, remember? Thing is, he's doing a lot better now. I mean, listen, the guy knows his shit. Say what you want, but he kept Morty Phillips alive."

"And that makes it okay?"

Sanders shrugged. "People change. Situations change. I hate to say this, man, but you're out of touch. Jorgenson —he's *with* us now."

"And I'm not?"

Sanders looked at me for a moment.

"No," he said. "I guess you're not."

Stiffly, like a stranger, Sanders moved across the hootch and lay down with a magazine and pretended to read.

I felt something shift inside me. It was anger, partly, but it was also a sense of pure and total loss: I didn't fit anymore. They were soldiers, I wasn't. In a few days they'd saddle up and head back into the bush, and I'd stand up on the helipad to watch them march away, and then after they were gone I'd spend the day loading resupply choppers until it was time to catch a movie or play cards or drink myself to sleep. A funny thing, but I felt betrayed.

For a long while I just stared at Mitchell Sanders.

"Loyalty," I said. "Such a pal."

In the morning I ran into Bobby Jorgenson. I was loading Hueys up on the helipad, and when the last bird took off, while I was putting on my shirt, I looked over and saw him leaning against my jeep, waiting for me. It was a surprise. He seemed smaller than I remembered, a little squirrel of a guy, short and stumpy-looking.

He nodded nervously.

"Well," he said.

At first I just looked down at his boots. Those boots: I remembered them from when I got shot. Out along the Song Tra Bong, a bullet inside me, all that pain, but for some reason what stuck to my memory was the unblemished leather of his fine new boots, factory fresh, no scuffs or dust or red clay. The boots were one of those vivid details you can't forget. Like a pebble or a blade of grass, you just stare and think, Dear Christ, there's the last thing on earth I'll ever see.

Jorgenson blinked and tried to smile. Oddly, I almost felt sympathy for him.

"Look," he said, "can we talk?"

I didn't move. I didn't say a word. Jorgenson's tongue flicked out, moving along the edge of his mustache, then slipped away.

"Listen, man, I fucked up," he said. "What else can I say? I'm sorry. When you got hit, I kept telling myself to move, move, but I couldn't *do* it, like I was full of drugs or something. You ever feel like that? Like you can't even move?"

"No," I said, "I never did."

"But can't you at least—"

"Excuses?"

Jorgenson's lip twitched. "No, I botched it. Period. Got all frozen up, I guess. The noise and shooting and everything—my first firefight—I just couldn't handle it . . . When I heard about the shock, the gangrene, I felt like . . . I felt miserable. Nightmares, too. I kept seeing you lying out there, heard you screaming, but it was like my legs were filled up with sand, they didn't *work*. I'd keep trying but I couldn't make my goddamn *legs* work."

He made a small sound in his throat, something low and feathery, and for a second I was afraid he might bawl. That would've ended it. I would've patted his shoulder and told him to forget it. But he kept control. He swallowed whatever the sound was and forced a smile and tried to shake my hand. It gave me an excuse to glare at him.

"It's not that easy," I said.

"Tim, I can't go back and do things over."

"My ass."

Jorgenson kept pushing his hand out at me. He looked so earnest, so sad and hurt, that it almost made me feel guilty. Not quite, though. After a second I muttered something and got into my jeep and put it to the floor and left him standing there.

I hated him for making me stop hating him.

Something had gone wrong. I'd come to this war a quiet, thoughtful sort of person, a college grad, Phi Beta Kappa and summa cum laude, all the credentials, but after seven months in the bush I realized that those high, civilized trappings had somehow been crushed under the weight of the simple daily realities. I'd turned mean inside. Even a little cruel at times. For all my education, all my fine liberal values, I now felt a deep coldness inside me, something dark and beyond reason. It's a hard thing to admit, even to myself, but I was capable of evil. I wanted to hurt Bobby Jorgenson the way he'd hurt me. For weeks it had been a vow—*I'll get him, I'll get him*—it was down inside me like a rock. Granted, I didn't hate him anymore, and I'd lost some of the outrage and passion, but the need for revenge kept eating at me. At night I sometimes drank too much. I'd remember getting shot and yelling out for a medic and then waiting and waiting and waiting, passing out once, then waking up and screaming some more, and how the screaming seemed to make new pain, the awful stink of myself, the sweat and fear, Bobby Jorgenson's clumsy fingers when he finally got around to working on me. I kept going over it all, every detail. I remembered the soft, fluid heat of my own blood. *Shock*, I thought, and I tried to tell him that, but my tongue wouldn't make the connection. I wanted to yell, "You jerk, it's shock—I'm *dying!*" but all I could do was whinny and squeal. I remembered that, and the hospital, and the nurses. I even remembered the rage. But I couldn't feel it anymore. In the end, all I felt was that coldness down inside my chest. Number one: the guy had almost killed me. Number two: there had to be consequences.

That afternoon I asked Mitchell Sanders to give me a hand.

"No pain," I said. "Basic psychology, that's all. Mess with his head a little."

"Negative," Sanders said.

"Spook the fucker."

Sanders shook his head. "Man, you're sick."

"All I want is—"

"Sick."

Quietly, Sanders looked at me for a second and then walked away.

I had to get Azar in on it.

He didn't have Mitchell Sanders's intelligence, but he had a keener sense of justice. After I explained the plan, Azar gave me a long white smile.

"Tonight?" he said.

"Just don't get carried away."

"Me?"

Still smiling, Azar flicked an eyebrow and started snapping his fingers. It was a tic of his. Whenever things got tense, whenever there was a prospect for action, he'd do that snapping thing. Nobody cared for him, including myself.

"Understand?" I said.

Azar winked. "Roger-dodger. Only a game, right?"


We called the enemy ghosts. "Bad night," we'd say, "the ghosts are out." To get spooked, in the lingo, meant not only to get scared but to get killed. "Don't get spooked," we'd say. "Stay cool, stay alive." Or we'd say: "Careful, man, don't give up the ghost." The countryside itself seemed spooky—shadows and tunnels and incense burning in the dark. The land was haunted. We were fighting forces that did not obey the laws of twentieth-century science. Late at night, on guard, it seemed that all of Vietnam was alive and shimmering—odd shapes swaying in the paddies, boogiemen in sandals, spirits dancing in old pagodas. It was ghost country, and Charlie Cong was the main ghost. The way he came out at night. How you never really saw him, just thought you did. Almost magical—appearing, disappearing. He could blend with the land, changing form, becoming trees and grass. He could levitate. He could fly. He could pass through barbed wire and melt away like ice and creep up on you without sound or footsteps. He was scary. In the daylight, maybe, you didn't believe in this stuff. You laughed it off. You made jokes. But at night you turned into a believer: no skeptics in foxholes.

Azar was wound up tight. All afternoon, while we made the preparations, he kept chanting, "Halloween, Halloween." That, plus the finger snapping, almost made me cancel the whole operation. I went hot and cold. Mitchell Sanders wouldn't speak to me, which tended to cool it off, but then I'd start remembering things. The result was a kind of numbness. No ice, no heat. I just went through the motions, rigidly, by the numbers, without any heart or real emotion. I rigged up my special effects, checked out the terrain, measured distances, collected the ordnance and equipment we'd need. I was professional enough about it, I didn't make mistakes, but somehow it felt as if I were gearing up to fight somebody else's war. I didn't have that patriotic zeal.

If there had been a dignified way out, I might've taken it. During evening chow, in fact, I kept staring across the mess hall at Bobby Jorgenson, and when he finally looked up at me, almost nodding, I came very close to calling it quits. Maybe I was fishing for something. One last apology—something public. But Jorgenson only gazed back at me. It was a strange gaze, too, straight on and unafraid, as if apologies were no longer required. He was sitting there with Dave Jensen and Mitchell Sanders and a few others, and he seemed to fit in very nicely, all chumminess and group rapport.

That's probably what cinched it.

I went back to my hootch, showered, shaved, threw my helmet against the wall, lay down for a while, got up, prowled around, talked to myself, applied some fresh ointment, then headed off to find Azar.

Just before dusk, Alpha Company stood for roll call. Afterward the men separated into two groups. Some went off to write letters or party or sleep; the others trooped down to the base perimeter, where, for the next eleven hours, they would pull night guard duty. It was SOP—one night on, one night off.

This was Jorgenson's night on. I knew that in advance, of course. And I knew his bunker assignment: Bunker Six, a pile of sandbags at the southwest corner of the perimeter. That morning I'd scouted out every inch of his position; I knew the blind spots and the little ripples of land and the places where he'd take cover in case of trouble. But still, just to guard against freak screw-ups, Azar and I tailed him down to the wire. We watched him lay out his poncho and connect his Claymores to their firing devices. Softly, like a little boy, he was whistling to himself. He tested his radio, unwrapped a candy bar, and sat back with his rifle cradled to his chest like a teddy bear.

"A pigeon," Azar whispered. "Roast pigeon on a spit. I smell it sizzling."

"Except this isn't for real."

Azar shrugged. After a second he reached out and clapped me on the shoulder, not roughly but not gently either. "What's real?" he said. "Eight months in fantasyland, it tends to blur the line. Honest to God, I sometimes can't remember what real *is*."

• • •

Psychology—that was one thing I knew. You don't try to scare people in broad daylight. You wait. Because the darkness squeezes you inside yourself, you get cut off from the outside world, the imagination takes over. That's basic psychology. I'd pulled enough night guard to know how the fear factor gets multiplied as you sit there hour after hour, nobody to talk to, nothing to do but stare into the big black hole at the center of your own sorry soul. The hours go by and you lose your gyroscope; your mind starts to roam. You think about dark closets, madmen, murderers under the bed, all those childhood fears. Gremlins and trolls and giants. You try to block it out but you can't. You see ghosts. You blink and shake your head. Bullshit, you tell yourself. But then you remember the guys who died: Curt Lemon, Kiowa, Ted Lavender, a half-dozen others whose faces you can't bring into focus anymore. And then pretty soon you start to ponder the stories you've heard about Charlie's magic. The time some guys cornered two VC in a dead-end tunnel, no way out, but how, when the tunnel was fragged and searched, nothing was found except a pile of dead rats. A hundred stories. Ghosts wiping out a whole squad of Marines in twenty seconds flat. Ghosts rising from the dead. Ghosts behind you and in front of you and inside you. After a while, as the night deepens, you feel a funny buzzing in your ears. Tiny sounds get heightened and distorted. The crickets talk in code; the night takes on an electronic tingle. You hold your breath. You coil up and tighten your muscles and listen, knuckles hard, the pulse ticking in your head. You hear the spooks laughing. No shit, *laughing*. You jerk up, you freeze, you squint at the dark. Nothing, though. You put your weapon on full automatic. You crouch lower and count your grenades and make sure the pins are bent for quick throwing and take a deep breath and listen and try not to freak. And then later, after enough time passes, things start to get bad.

"Come on," Azar said, "let's *do it*," but I told him to be patient. Waiting was the trick. So we went to the movies, *Barbarella* again, the eighth straight night. A lousy movie, I thought, but it kept Azar occupied. He was crazy about Jane Fonda. "Sweet Janie," he kept saying. "Sweet Janie boosts a man's morale." Then, with his hand, he showed me which part of his morale got boosted. It was an old joke. Everything was old. The movie, the heat, the booze, the war. I fell asleep during the second reel—a hot, angry sleep—and forty minutes later I woke up to a sore ass and a foul temper.

It wasn't yet midnight.

We hiked over to the EM club and worked our way through a six-pack. Mitchell Sanders was there, at another table, but he pretended not to see me.

Around closing time, I nodded at Azar.

"Well, goody gum drop," he said.

We went over to my hootch, picked up our gear, and then moved through the night down to the wire. I felt like a soldier again. Back in the bush, it seemed. We observed good field discipline, not talking, keeping to the shadows and joining in with the darkness. When we came up on Bunker Six, Azar lifted his thumb and peeled away from me and began circling to the south. Old times, I thought. A kind of thrill, a kind of dread.

Quietly, I shouldered my gear and crossed over to a heap of boulders that overlooked Jorgenson's position. I was directly behind him. Thirty-two meters away, exactly. Even in the heavy darkness, no moon yet, I could make out the kid's silhouette: a helmet, a pair of shoulders, a rifle barrel. His back was to me. He gazed out at the wire and at the paddies beyond, where the danger was.

I knelt down and took out ten flares and unscrewed the caps and lined them up in front of me and then checked my wristwatch. Still five minutes to go. Edging over to my left, I groped for the ropes I'd set up that afternoon. I found them, tested the tension, and checked the time again. Four minutes. There was a light feeling in my head, fluttery and taut at the same time. I remembered it from the boonies. Giddiness and doubt and awe, all those things and a million more. It's as if you're in a movie. There's a camera on you, so you begin acting, you're somebody else. You think of all the films you've seen, Audie Murphy and Gary Cooper and the Cisco Kid, all those heroes, and you can't help falling back on them as models of proper comportment. On ambush, curled in the dark, you fight for control. Not too much fidgeting. You rearrange your posture; you measure out your breathing. Eyes open, be alert—old imperatives, old movies. It all swirls together, clichés mixing with your own emotions, and in the end you can't tell one from the other.

There was that coldness inside me. I wasn't myself. I felt hollow and dangerous.

I took a breath, fingered the first rope, and gave it a sharp little jerk. Instantly there was a clatter outside the wire. I expected the noise, I was even tensed for it, but still my heart took a hop.

Now, I thought. Now it starts.

Eight ropes altogether. I had four, Azar had four. Each rope was hooked up to a homemade noisemaker out in front of Jorgenson's bunker—eight ammo cans filled with rifle cartridges. Simple devices, but they worked. I waited a moment, and then, very gently, I gave all four of my ropes a little tug. Delicate, nothing loud. If you weren't listening, listening hard, you might've missed it. But Jorgenson was listening. At the first low rattle, his silhouette seemed to freeze.

Another rattle: Azar this time. We kept at it for ten minutes, staggering the rhythm — noise, silence, noise — gradually building the tension.

Squinting down at Jorgenson's position, I felt a swell of immense power. It was a feeling the VC must have. Like a puppeteer. Yank on the ropes, watch the silly wooden soldier jump and twitch. One by one, in sequence, I tugged on each of the ropes, and the sounds came flowing back at me with a soft, indefinite formlessness: a rattlesnake, maybe, or the creak of a trap door, or footsteps in the attic — whatever you made of it.

In a way I wanted to stop myself. It was cruel, I knew that, but right and wrong were somewhere else.

I heard myself chuckle.

And then presently I came unattached from the natural world. I felt the hinges go. Eyes closed, I seemed to rise up out of my own body and float through the dark down to Jorgenson's position. I was invisible; I had no shape, no substance; I weighed less than nothing. I just drifted. It was imagination, of course, but for a long while I hovered there over Bobby Jorgenson's bunker. As if through dark glass I could see him lying flat in his circle of sandbags, silent and scared, listening, telling himself it was all a trick of the dark. Muscles tight, ears tight — I could *see* it. Now, at this instant, he'd glance up at the sky, hoping for a moon or a few stars.

But no moon, no stars. He'd start talking to himself. He'd try to bring the night into focus, willing coherence, but the effort would only cause distortions. Out beyond the wire, the paddies would seem to swirl and sway; the trees would take human form; clumps of grass would glide through the night like sappers. Funhouse country: trick mirrors and curvatures and pop-up monsters. "Take it easy," he'd murmur, "easy, easy, easy," but it wouldn't get any easier.

I could actually see it.

I was down there with him, inside him. I was part of the night. I was the land itself—everything, everywhere—the fireflies and paddies, the midnight rustlings, the cool phosphorescent shimmer of evil—I was atrocity—I was jungle fire, jungle drums—I was the blind stare in the eyes of all those poor, dead, dumbfuck ex-pals of mine—all the pale young corpses, Lee Strunk and Kiowa and Curt Lemon—I was the beast on their lips—I was Nam—the horror, the war.

"Creepy," Azar said. "Wet pants an' goose bumps." He held a beer out to me, but I shook my head.

We sat in the dim light of my hootch, boots off, listening to Mary Hopkin on my tape deck.

"What next?"

"Wait," I said.

"Sure, but I mean—"

"Shut up and *listen*."

That high elegant voice. Someday, when the war was over, I'd go to London and ask Mary Hopkin to marry me. That's another thing Nam does to you. It turns you sentimental; it makes you want to hook up with girls like Mary

Hopkin. You learn, finally, that you'll die, and so you try to hang on to your own life, that gentle, naive kid you used to be, but then after a while the sentiment takes over, and the sadness, because you know for a fact that you can't ever bring any of it back again. You just can't. Those were the days, she sang.

Azar switched off the tape.

"Shit, man," he said. "Don't you got *music?*"

And now, finally, the moon was out. We slipped back to our positions and went to work again with the ropes. Louder now, more insistent. Starlight sparkled in the barbed wire, and there were curious reflections and layerings of shadow, and the big white moon added resonance. There was nothing moral in the world. The night was absolute. Slowly, we dragged the ammo cans closer to Bobby Jorgenson's bunker, and this, plus the moon, gave a sense of approaching peril, the slow belly-down crawl of evil.

At 0300 hours Azar set off the first trip flare.

There was a light popping noise, then a sizzle out in front of Bunker Six. The night seemed to snap itself in half. The white flare burned ten paces from the bunker.

I fired off three more flares and it was instant daylight.

Then Jorgenson moved. He made a short, low cry—not even a cry, really, just a short lung-and-throat bark—and there was a blurred sequence as he lunged sideways and rolled toward a heap of sandbags and crouched there and hugged his rifle and waited.

"There," I whispered. "Now you know."

I could read his mind. I was there with him. Together we understood what terror was: you're not human anymore.

You're a shadow. You slip out of your own skin, like molting, shedding your own history and your own future, leaving behind everything you ever were or wanted or believed in. You know you're about to die. And it's not a movie and you aren't a hero and all you can do is whimper and wait.

This, now, was something we shared.

I felt close to him. It wasn't compassion, just closeness. His silhouette was framed like a cardboard cutout against the burning flares.

In the dark outside my hootch, even though I bent toward him, almost nose to nose, all I could see were the glossy whites of Azar's eyes.

"Enough," I said.

"Oh, sure."

"Seriously."

Azar gave me a small, thin smile.

"Serious?" he said. "That's way too serious for me—I'm your basic fun lover."

When he smiled again, I knew it was hopeless, but I tried anyway. I told him the score was even. We'd made our point, I said, no need to rub it in.

Azar stared at me.

"Poor, poor boy," he said. The rest was inflection and white eyes.

An hour before dawn we moved in for the last phase. Azar was in command now. I tagged after him, thinking maybe I could keep a lid on.

"Don't take this personal," Azar said cheerfully. "It's my own character flaw. I just like to finish things."

I didn't look at him. As we approached the wire, Azar put his hand on my shoulder, guiding me over toward the boulder pile. He knelt down and inspected the ropes and flares, nodded to himself, peered out at Jorgenson's bunker, nodded once more, then took off his helmet and sat on it.

He was smiling again.

"You know something?" he said. His voice was wistful. "Out here, at night, I almost feel like a kid again. The Vietnam experience. I mean, wow, I *love* this shit."

"Let's just—"

"Shhhh."

Azar put a finger to his lips. He was still smiling at me, almost kindly.

"This here's what you wanted," he said. "You dig playing war, right? That's all this *is*. A cute little backyard war game. Brings back memories, I bet—those happy soldiering days. Except now you're a has-been. One of those American Legion types, guys who like to dress up in a nifty uniform and go out and play at it. Pitiful. It was me, I'd rather get my ass blown away for real."

My lips had a waxy feel, like soapstone.

"Come on," I said. "Just quit."

"Pitiful."

"Azar, for Christ sake."

He patted my cheek. "Purely pitiful," he said.

We waited another ten minutes. It was cold now, and damp. Squatting down, I felt a brittleness come over me, a hollow sensation, as if someone could reach out and crush me like a Christmas tree ornament. It was the same feeling I'd had out along the Song Tra Bong. Like I was losing myself, everything spilling out. I remembered how the bullet had made a soft puffing noise inside me. I remembered lying there for a long while, listening to the river, the gunfire and voices, how I kept calling out for a medic but how nobody came and how I finally reached back and touched the hole. The blood was warm like dishwater. I could feel my pants filling up with it. All this blood, I thought—I'll be *hollow*. Then the brittle sensation hit me. I passed out for a while, and when I woke up the battle had moved farther down the river. I was still leaking. I wondered where Rat Kiley was, but Rat Kiley was in Japan. There was rifle fire somewhere off to my right, and people yelling, except none of it seemed real anymore. I smelled myself dying. The round had entered at a steep angle, smashing down through the hip and colon. The stench made me jerk sideways. I turned and clamped a hand against the wound and tried to plug it up. Leaking to death, I thought. Like a genie swirling out of a bottle—like a cloud of gas—I was drifting upward out of my own body. I was half in and half out. Part of me still lay there, the corpse part, but I was also that genie looking on and saying, "There, there," which made me start to scream. I couldn't help it. When Bobby Jorgenson got to me, I was almost gone with shock. All I could do was scream. I tightened up and squeezed, trying to stop the leak, but that only made it worse, and Jorgenson punched me and told me to knock it off. Shock, I thought. I tried to tell him that. I tried to say, "Shock," but it wouldn't come out right. Jorgenson flipped me over and pressed a knee against my back, pinning me there, and I kept trying to say, "Shock, man, treat for shock." I was lucid—things were clear—but my tongue wouldn't fit around the words. Then I slipped under for a while. When I came back, Jorgenson was using a knife to cut off my pants.

He shot in the morphine, which scared me, and I shouted something and tried to wiggle away, but he kept pushing down hard on my back. Except it wasn't Jorgenson now—it was that genie—he was smiling down at me, and winking, and I couldn't buck him off. Later on, things clicked into slow motion. The morphine, maybe. I focused on Jorgenson's brand-new boots, then on a pebble, then on my own face floating high above me—the last things I'd ever see. I couldn't look away. It occurred to me that I was witness to something rare.

Even now, in the dark, there were indications of a spirit world.

Azar said, "Hey, you awake?"

I nodded.

Down at Bunker Six, things were silent. The place looked abandoned.

Azar grinned and went to work on the ropes. It began like a breeze, a soft sighing sound. I hugged myself. I watched Azar bend forward and fire off the first illumination flare. "Please," I almost said, but the word snagged, and I looked up and tracked the flare over Jorgenson's bunker. It exploded almost without noise: a soft red flash.

There was a whimper in the dark. At first I thought it was Jorgenson.

"Please?" I said.

I bit down and folded my hands and squeezed. I had the shivers.

Twice more, rapidly, Azar fired up red flares. At one point he turned toward me and lifted his eyebrows.

"Timmy, Timmy," he said. "Such a specimen."

I agreed.

I wanted to do something, stop him somehow, but I crouched back and watched Azar pick up a tear-gas grenade and pull the pin and stand up and throw. The gas puffed up in a thin cloud that partly obscured Bunker Six. Even from thirty meters away I could smell it and taste it.

"Jesus, *please*," I said, but Azar lobbed over another one, waited for the hiss, then scrambled over to the rope we hadn't used yet.

It was my idea. I'd rigged it up myself: a sandbag painted white, a pulley system.

Azar gave the rope a quick tug, and out in front of Bunker Six, the white sandbag lifted itself up and hovered there in a misty swirl of gas.

Jorgenson began firing. Just one round at first, a single red tracer that thumped into the sandbag and burned.

"Oooo!" Azar murmured.

Quickly, talking to himself, Azar hurled the last gas grenade, shot up another flare, then snatched the rope again and made the white sandbag dance.

"Oooo!" he was chanting. "Star light, star bright!"

Bobby Jorgenson did not go nuts. Quietly, almost with dignity, he stood up and took aim and fired once more at the sandbag. I could see his profile against the red flares. His face seemed relaxed. He stared out into the dark for several seconds, as if deciding something, then he shook his head and began marching out toward the wire. His posture was erect; he did not crouch or squirm or crawl. He walked upright. He moved with a kind of grace. When he reached the sandbag, Jorgenson stopped and turned and shouted out my name, then he placed his rifle muzzle up against the white sandbag.

"O'Brien!" he yelled, and he fired.

Azar dropped the rope.

"Well," he muttered, "show's over." He looked down at me with a mixture of contempt and pity. After a second he shook his head. "Man, I'll tell you something. You're a sorry, sorry case."

I was trembling. I kept hugging myself, rocking, but I couldn't make it go away.

"Disgusting," Azar said. "Sorriest fuckin' specimen I ever seen."

He looked out at Jorgenson, then at me. His eyes had the opaque, spiritless surface of stone. He moved forward as if to help me up. Then he stopped. Almost as an afterthought, he kicked me in the head.

"Sad," he murmured, and headed off to bed.

"No big deal," I told Jorgenson. "Leave it alone."

But he led me down to the bunker and used a towel to wipe the gash at my forehead. It wasn't bad, really. I felt some dizziness, but I tried not to let it show.

It was almost dawn now. For a while we didn't speak.

"So," he finally said.

"Right."

We shook hands. Neither of us put much emotion into it and we didn't look at each other's eyes.

Jorgenson pointed out at the shot-up sandbag.

"That was a nice touch," he said. "It almost had me—" He paused and squinted out at the eastern paddies, where the sky was beginning to color up. "Anyway, a nice dramatic touch. Someday maybe you should go into the movies or something."

I nodded and said, "That's an idea."

"Another Hitchcock. *The Birds*—you ever see it?"

"Scary stuff," I said.

We sat for a while longer, then I started to get up, except I was still feeling the wobbles in my head. Jorgenson reached out and steadied me.

"We're even now?" he said.

"Pretty much."

Again, I felt that closeness. Almost war buddies. We nearly shook hands again but then decided against it. Jorgenson picked up his helmet, brushed it off, and looked back one more time at the white sandbag. His face was filthy.

Up at the medic's hootch, he cleaned and bandaged my forehead, then we went to chow. We didn't have much to say. I told him I was sorry; he told me the same thing. Afterward, in an awkward moment, I said, "Let's kill Azar."

Jorgenson gave me a half-grin. "Scare him to death, right?"

"Right," I said.

"What a movie!"

I shrugged. "Sure. Or just kill him."

# Night Life

A few words about Rat Kiley. I wasn't there when he got hurt, but Mitchell Sanders later told me the essential facts. Apparently he lost his cool.

The platoon had been working an AO out in the foothills west of Quang Ngai City, and for some time they'd been receiving intelligence about an NVA buildup in the area. The usual crazy rumors: massed artillery and Russian tanks and whole divisions of fresh troops. No one took it seriously, including Lieutenant Cross, but as a precaution the platoon moved only at night, staying off the main trails and observing strict field SOPs. For almost two weeks, Sanders said, they lived the night life. That was the phrase everyone used: the night life. A language trick. It made things seem tolerable. How's the Nam treating you? one guy would ask, and some other guy would say, Hey, one big party, just living the night life.

It was a tense time for everybody, Sanders said, but for Rat Kiley it ended up in Japan. The strain was too much for him. He couldn't make the adjustment.

During those two weeks the basic routine was simple. They'd sleep away the daylight hours, or try to sleep, then at dusk they'd put on their gear and move out single file into the dark. Always a heavy cloud cover. No moon and no stars. It was the purest black you could imagine, Sanders said, the kind of clock-stopping black that God must've had in mind when he sat down to invent blackness. It made your eyeballs ache. You'd shake your head and blink, except you couldn't even tell you were blinking, the blackness didn't change. So pretty soon you'd get jumpy. Your nerves would go. You'd start to worry about getting cut off from the rest of the unit—alone, you'd think—and then the real panic would bang in and you'd reach out and try to touch the guy in front of you, groping for his shirt, hoping to Christ he was still there. It made for some bad dreams. Dave Jensen popped special vitamins high in carotene. Lieutenant Cross popped NoDoz. Henry Dobbins and Norman Bowker even rigged up a safety line between them, a long piece of wire tied to their belts. The whole platoon felt the impact.

With Rat Kiley, though, it was different. Too many body bags, maybe. Too much gore.

At first Rat just sank inside himself, not saying a word, but then later on, after five or six days, it flipped the other way. He couldn't stop talking. Wacky talk, too. Talking about bugs, for instance: how the worst thing in Nam was the goddamn bugs. Big giant killer bugs, he'd say, mutant bugs, bugs with fucked-up DNA, bugs that were chemically altered by napalm and defoliants and tear gas and DDT. He claimed the bugs were personally after his ass. He said he could hear the bastards homing in on him. Swarms of mutant bugs, billions of them, they had him bracketed. Whispering his name, he said—his actual name—all night long—it was driving him crazy.

Odd stuff, Sanders said, and it wasn't just talk. Rat developed some peculiar habits. Constantly scratching himself. Clawing at the bug bites. He couldn't quit digging at his skin, making big scabs and then ripping off the scabs and scratching the open sores.

It was a sad thing to watch. Definitely not the old Rat Kiley. His whole personality seemed out of kilter.

To an extent, though, everybody was feeling it. The long night marches turned their minds upside down; all the rhythms were wrong. Always a lost sensation. They'd blunder along through the dark, willy-nilly, no sense of place or direction, probing for an enemy that nobody could see. Like a snipe hunt, Sanders said. A bunch of dumb Cub Scouts chasing the phantoms. They'd march north for a time, then east, then north again, skirting the villages, no one talking except in whispers. And it was rugged country, too. Not quite mountains, but rising fast, full of gorges and deep brush and places you could die. Around midnight things always got wild. All around you, everywhere, the whole dark countryside came alive. You'd hear a strange hum in your ears. Nothing specific; nothing you could put a name on. Tree frogs, maybe, or snakes or flying squirrels or who-knew-what. Like the night had its own voice—that hum in your ears—and in the hours after midnight you'd swear you were walking through some kind of soft black protoplasm, Vietnam, the blood and the flesh.

It was no joke, Sanders said. The monkeys chattered death-chatter. The nights got freaky.

Rat Kiley finally hit a wall.

He couldn't sleep during the hot daylight hours; he couldn't cope with the nights.

Late one afternoon, as the platoon prepared for another march, he broke down in front of Mitchell Sanders. Not crying, but up against it. He said he was scared. And it wasn't normal scared. He didn't know *what* it was: too long in-country, probably. Or else he wasn't cut out to be a medic. Always policing up the parts, he said. Always plugging up holes. Sometimes he'd stare at guys who were still okay, the alive guys, and he'd start to picture how they'd look dead. Without arms or legs—that sort of thing. It was ghoulish, he knew that, but he couldn't shut off the pictures. He'd be sitting there talking with Bowker or Dobbins or somebody, just marking time, and then out of nowhere he'd find himself wondering how much the guy's head weighed, like how *heavy* it was, and what it would feel like to pick up the head and carry it over to a chopper and dump it in.

Rat scratched the skin at his elbow, digging in hard. His eyes were red and weary.

"It's not right," he said. "These pictures in my head, they won't quit. I'll see a guy's liver. The actual fucking *liver*. And the thing is, it doesn't scare me, it doesn't even give me the willies. More like curiosity. The way a doctor feels when he looks at a patient, sort of mechanical, not seeing the real person, just a ruptured appendix or a clogged-up artery."

His voice floated away for a second. He looked at Sanders and tried to smile.

He kept clawing at his elbow.

"Anyway," Rat said, "the days aren't so bad, but at night the pictures get to be a bitch. I start seeing my own body. Chunks of myself. My own heart, my own kidneys. It's like

—I don't know—it's like staring into this huge black crystal ball. One of these nights I'll be lying dead out there in the dark and nobody'll find me except the bugs—I can *see* it—I can see the goddamn bugs chewing tunnels through me—I can see the mongooses munching on my bones. I swear, it's too much. I can't keep seeing myself dead."

Mitchell Sanders nodded. He didn't know what to say. For a time they sat watching the shadows come, then Rat shook his head.

He said he'd done his best. He'd tried to be a decent medic. Win some and lose some, he said, but he'd tried hard. Briefly then, rambling a little, he talked about a few of the guys who were gone now, Curt Lemon and Kiowa and Ted Lavender, and how crazy it was that people who were so incredibly alive could get so incredibly dead.

Then he almost laughed.

"This whole war," he said. "You know what it is? Just one big banquet. Meat, man. You and me. Everybody. Meat for the bugs."

The next morning he shot himself.

He took off his boots and socks, laid out his medical kit, doped himself up, and put a round through his foot.

Nobody blamed him, Sanders said.

Before the chopper came, there was time for goodbyes. Lieutenant Cross went over and said he'd vouch that it was an accident. Henry Dobbins and Azar gave him a stack of comic books for hospital reading. Everybody stood in a little circle, feeling bad about it, trying to cheer him up with bullshit about the great night life in Japan.

# The Lives of the Dead

**B**ut this too is true: stories can save us. I'm forty-three years old, and a writer now, and even still, right here, I keep dreaming Linda alive. And Ted Lavender, too, and Kiowa, and Curt Lemon, and a slim young man I killed, and an old man sprawled beside a pigpen, and several others whose bodies I once lifted and dumped into a truck. They're all dead. But in a story, which is a kind of dreaming, the dead sometimes smile and sit up and return to the world.

Start here: a body without a name. On an afternoon in 1969 the platoon took sniper fire from a filthy little village along the South China Sea. It lasted only a minute or two, and nobody was hurt, but even so Lieutenant Jimmy Cross got on the radio and ordered up an air strike. For the next half hour we watched the place burn. It was a cool bright morning, like early autumn, and the jets were glossy black against the sky. When it ended, we formed into a loose line and swept east through the village. It was all wreckage. I remember the smell of burnt straw; I remember broken fences and torn-up trees and heaps of stone and brick and pottery. The place was deserted—no people, no animals—and the only confirmed kill was an old man who lay face-up near a pigpen at the center of the village. His right arm was gone. At his face there were already many flies and gnats.

Dave Jensen went over and shook the old man's hand. "How-dee-doo," he said.

One by one the others did it too. They didn't disturb the body, they just grabbed the old man's hand and offered a few words and moved away.

Rat Kiley bent over the corpse. "Gimme five," he said. "A real honor."

"Pleased as punch," said Henry Dobbins.

I was brand-new to the war. It was my fourth day; I hadn't yet developed a sense of humor. Right away, as if I'd swallowed something, I felt a moist sickness rise up in my throat. I sat down beside the pigpen, closed my eyes, put my head between my knees.

After a moment Dave Jensen touched my shoulder.

"Be polite now," he said. "Go introduce yourself. Nothing to be afraid about, just a nice old man. Show a little respect for your elders."

"No way."

"Maybe it's too real for you?"

"That's right," I said. "Way too real."

Jensen kept after me, but I didn't go near the body. I didn't even look at it except by accident. For the rest of the day there was still that sickness inside me, but it wasn't the old man's corpse so much, it was that awesome act of greeting the dead. At one point, I remember, they sat the body up against a fence. They crossed his legs and talked to him. "The guest of honor," Mitchell Sanders said, and he placed a can of orange slices in the old man's lap. "Vitamin C," he said gently. "A guy's health, that's the most important thing."

They proposed toasts. They lifted their canteens and drank to the old man's family and ancestors, his many grandchildren, his newfound life after death. It was more than mockery. There was a formality to it, like a funeral without the sadness.

Dave Jensen flicked his eyes at me.

"Hey, O'Brien," he said, "you got a toast in mind? Never too late for manners."

I found things to do with my hands. I looked away and tried not to think.

Late in the afternoon, just before dusk, Kiowa came up and asked if he could sit at my foxhole for a minute. He offered me a Christmas cookie from a batch his father had sent him. It was February now, but the cookies tasted fine.

For a few moments Kiowa watched the sky.

"You did a good thing today," he said. "That shaking hands crap, it isn't decent. The guys'll hassle you for a while—especially Jensen—but just keep saying no. Should've done it myself. Takes guts, I know that."

"It wasn't guts. I was scared."

Kiowa shrugged. "Same difference."

"No, I couldn't *do* it. A mental block or something . . . I don't know, just creepy."

"Well, you're new here. You'll get used to it." He paused for a second, studying the green and red sprinkles on a cookie. "Today—I guess this was your first look at a real body?"

I shook my head. All day long I'd been picturing Linda's face, the way she smiled.

"It sounds funny," I said, "but that poor old man, he reminds me of . . . I mean, there's this girl I used to know. I took her to the movies once. My first date."

Kiowa looked at me for a long while. Then he leaned back and smiled.

"Man," he said, "that's a bad date."

Linda was nine then, as I was, but we were in love. And it was real. When I write about her now, three decades later, it's tempting to dismiss it as a crush, an infatuation of childhood, but I know for a fact that what we felt for each other was as deep and rich as love can ever get. It had all the shadings and complexities of mature adult love, and maybe more, because there were not yet words for it, and because it was not yet fixed to comparisons or chronologies or the ways by which adults measure such things.

I just loved her.

She had poise and great dignity. Her eyes, I remember, were deep brown like her hair, and she was slender and very quiet and fragile-looking.

Even then, at nine years old, I wanted to live inside her body. I wanted to melt into her bones—*that* kind of love.

And so in the spring of 1956, when we were in the fourth grade, I took her out on the first real date of my life—a double date, actually, with my mother and father. Though I can't remember the exact sequence, my mother had somehow arranged it with Linda's parents, and on that damp spring night my dad did the driving while Linda and I sat in the back seat and stared out opposite windows, both of us trying to pretend it was nothing special. For me, though, it was very special. Down inside I had important things to tell her, big profound things, but I couldn't make any words come out. I had trouble breathing. Now and then I'd glance over at her, thinking how beautiful she was: her white skin and those dark brown eyes and the way she always smiled at the world—always, it seemed—as if her face had been designed that way. The smile never went away. That night, I remember, she wore a new red cap, which seemed to me very stylish and sophisticated, very unusual. It was a stocking cap, basically, except the tapered part at the top seemed extra long, almost too long, like a tail growing out of the back of her head. It made me think of the caps that Santa's elves wear, the same shape and color, the same fuzzy white tassel at the tip.

Sitting there in the back seat, I wanted to find some way to let her know how I felt, a compliment of some sort, but all I could manage was a stupid comment about the cap. "Jeez," I must've said, "what a *cap*."

Linda smiled at the window—she knew what I meant —but my mother turned and gave me a hard look. It surprised me. It was as if I'd brought up some horrible secret.

For the rest of the ride I kept my mouth shut. We parked in front of the Ben Franklin store and walked up Main Street toward the State Theater. My parents went first, side by side, and then Linda in her new red cap, and then me tailing along ten or twenty steps behind. I was nine years old; I didn't yet have the gift for small talk. Now and then my mother glanced back, making little motions with her hand to speed me up.

At the ticket booth, I remember, Linda stood off to one side. I moved over to the concession area, studying the candy, and both of us were very careful to avoid the awkwardness of eye contact. Which was how we knew about being in love. It was pure knowing. Neither of us, I suppose, would've thought to use that word, love, but by the fact of not looking at each other, and not talking, we understood with a clarity beyond language that we were sharing something huge and permanent.

Behind me, in the theater, I heard cartoon music.

"Hey, step it up," I said. I almost had the courage to look at her. "You want popcorn or *what?*"

The thing about a story is that you dream it as you tell it, hoping that others might then dream along with you, and in this way memory and imagination and language combine to make spirits in the head. There is the illusion of aliveness. In Vietnam, for instance, Ted Lavender had a habit of popping four or five tranquilizers every morning. It was his way of coping, just dealing with the realities, and the drugs helped to ease him through the days. I remember how peaceful his eyes were. Even in bad situations he had a soft, dreamy expression on his face, which was what he wanted, a kind of escape. "How's the war today?" somebody would ask, and Ted Lavender would give a little smile to the sky and say, "Mellow—a nice smooth war today." And then in April he was shot in the head outside the village of Than Khe. Kiowa and I and a couple of others were ordered to prepare his body for the dustoff. I remember squatting down, not wanting to look but then looking. Lavender's left cheekbone was gone. There was a swollen blackness around his eye. Quickly, trying not to feel anything, we went through the kid's pockets. I remember wishing I had gloves. It wasn't the blood I hated; it was the deadness. We put his personal effects in a plastic bag and tied the bag to his arm. We stripped off the canteens and ammo, all the heavy stuff, and wrapped him up in his own poncho and carried him out to a dry paddy and laid him down.

For a while nobody said much. Then Mitchell Sanders laughed and looked over at the green plastic poncho.

"Hey, Lavender," he said, "how's the war today?"

There was a short quiet.

"Mellow," somebody said.

"Well, that's good," Sanders murmured, "that's real, real good. Stay cool now."

"Hey, no sweat, I'm mellow."

"Just ease on back, then. Don't need no pills. We got this incredible chopper on call, this once in a lifetime mind-trip."

"Oh, yeah—mellow!"

Mitchell Sanders smiled. "There it is, my man, this chopper gonna take you up high and cool. Gonna relax you. Gonna alter your whole perspective on this sorry, sorry shit."

We could almost see Ted Lavender's dreamy blue eyes. We could almost hear him.

"Roger that," somebody said. "I'm ready to fly."

There was the sound of the wind, the sound of birds and the quiet afternoon, which was the world we were in.

That's what a story does. The bodies are animated. You make the dead talk. They sometimes say things like, "Roger that." Or they say, "Timmy, stop crying," which is what Linda said to me after she was dead.

Even now I can see her walking down the aisle of the old State Theater in Worthington, Minnesota. I can see her face in profile beside me, the cheeks softly lighted by coming attractions.

The movie that night was *The Man Who Never Was.* I remember the plot clearly, or at least the premise, because the main character was a corpse. That fact alone, I know, deeply impressed me. It was a World War Two film: the Allies devise a scheme to mislead Germany about the site of the upcoming landings in Europe. They get their hands on a body—a British soldier, I believe; they dress him up in an officer's uniform, plant fake documents in his pockets, then dump him in the sea and let the currents wash him onto a Nazi beach. The Germans find the documents; the deception wins the war. Even now, I can remember the awful splash as that corpse fell into the sea. I remember glancing over at Linda, thinking it might be too much for her, but in the dim gray light she seemed to be smiling at the screen. There were little crinkles at her eyes, her lips open and gently curving at the corners. I couldn't understand it. There was nothing to smile at. Once or twice, in fact, I had to close my eyes, but it didn't help much. Even then I kept seeing the soldier's body tumbling toward the water, splashing down hard, how inert and heavy it was, how completely dead.

It was a relief when the movie finally ended.

Afterward, we drove out to the Dairy Queen at the edge of town. The night had a quilted, weighted-down quality, as if somehow burdened, and all around us the Minnesota prairies reached out in long repetitive waves of corn and soybeans, everything flat, everything the same. I remember eating ice cream in the back seat of the Buick, and a long blank drive in the dark, and then pulling up in front of Linda's house. Things must've been said, but it's all gone now except for a few last images. I remember walking her to the front door. I remember the brass porch light with its fierce yellow glow, my own feet, the juniper bushes along the front steps, the wet grass, Linda close beside me. We were in love. Nine years old, yes, but it was real love, and now we were alone on those front steps. Finally we looked at each other.

"Bye," I said.

Linda nodded and said, "Bye."

Over the next few weeks Linda wore her new red cap to school every day. She never took it off, not even in the classroom, and so it was inevitable that she took some teasing about it. Most of it came from a kid named Nick Veenhof. Out on the playground, during recess, Nick would creep up behind her and make a grab for the cap, almost yanking it off, then scampering away. It went on like that for weeks: the girls giggling, the guys egging him on. Naturally I wanted to do something about it, but it just wasn't possible. I had my reputation to think about. I had my pride. And there was also the problem of Nick Veenhof. So I stood off to the side, just a spectator, wishing I could do things I couldn't do. I watched Linda clamp down the cap with the palm of her hand, holding it there, smiling over in Nick's direction as if none of it really mattered.

For me, though, it did matter. It still does. I should've stepped in; fourth grade is no excuse. Besides, it doesn't get easier with time, and twelve years later, when Vietnam presented much harder choices, some practice at being brave might've helped a little.

Also, too, I might've stopped what happened next. Maybe not, but at least it's possible.

Most of the details I've forgotten, or maybe blocked out, but I know it was an afternoon in late spring, and we were

taking a spelling test, and halfway into the test Nick Veenhof held up his hand and asked to use the pencil sharpener.
Right away a couple of kids laughed. No doubt he'd broken
the pencil on purpose, but it wasn't something you could
prove, and so the teacher nodded and told him to hustle it
up. Which was a mistake. Out of nowhere Nick developed
a terrible limp. He moved in slow motion, dragging himself
up to the pencil sharpener and carefully slipping in his pencil and then grinding away forever. At the time, I suppose, it
was funny. But on the way back to his seat Nick took a short
detour. He squeezed between two desks, turned sharply
right, and moved up the aisle toward Linda.

I saw him grin at one of his pals. In a way, I already knew
what was coming.

As he passed Linda's desk, he dropped the pencil and
squatted down to get it. When he came up, his left hand
slipped behind her back. There was a half-second hesita-
tion. Maybe he was trying to stop himself; maybe then, just
briefly, he felt some small approximation of guilt. But it
wasn't enough. He took hold of the white tassel, stood up,
and gently lifted off her cap.

Somebody must've laughed. I remember a short, tinny
echo. I remember Nick Veenhof trying to smile. Somewhere
behind me, a girl said, "Uh," or a sound like that.

Linda didn't move.

Even now, when I think back on it, I can still see the
glossy whiteness of her scalp. She wasn't bald. Not quite.
Not completely. There were some tufts of hair, little patches
of grayish brown fuzz. But what I saw then, and keep seeing
now, is all that whiteness. A smooth, pale, translucent white.
I could see the bones and veins; I could see the exact structure of her skull. There was a large Band-Aid at the back

of her head, a row of black stitches, a piece of gauze taped above her left ear.

Nick Veenhof took a step backward. He was still smiling, but the smile was doing strange things.

The whole time Linda stared straight ahead, her eyes locked on the blackboard, her hands loosely folded at her lap. She didn't say anything. After a time, though, she turned and looked at me across the room. It lasted only a moment, but I had the feeling that a whole conversation was happening between us. *Well?* she was saying, and I was saying, *Sure, okay.*

Later on, she cried for a while. The teacher helped her put the cap back on, then we finished the spelling test and did some fingerpainting, and after school that day Nick Veenhof and I walked her home.

It's now 1990. I'm forty-three years old, which would've seemed impossible to a fourth grader, and yet when I look at photographs of myself as I was in 1956, I realize that in the important ways I haven't changed at all. I was Timmy then; now I'm Tim. But the essence remains the same. I'm not fooled by the baggy pants or the crew cut or the happy smile—I know my own eyes—and there is no doubt that the Timmy smiling at the camera is the Tim I am now. Inside the body, or beyond the body, there is something absolute and unchanging. The human life is all one thing, like a blade tracing loops on ice: a little kid, a twenty-three-year-old infantry sergeant, a middle-aged writer knowing guilt and sorrow.

And as a writer now, I want to save Linda's life. Not her body—her life.

She died, of course. Nine years old and she died. It was

a brain tumor. She lived through the summer and into the first part of September, and then she was dead.

But in a story I can steal her soul. I can revive, at least briefly, that which is absolute and unchanging. In a story, miracles can happen. Linda can smile and sit up. She can reach out, touch my wrist, and say, "Timmy, stop crying."

I needed that kind of miracle. At some point I had come to understand that Linda was sick, maybe even dying, but I loved her and just couldn't accept it. In the middle of the summer, I remember, my mother tried to explain to me about brain tumors. Now and then, she said, bad things start growing inside us. Sometimes you can cut them out and other times you can't, and for Linda it was one of the times when you can't.

I thought about it for several days. "All right," I finally said. "So will she get better now?"

"Well, no," my mother said, "I don't think so." She stared at a spot behind my shoulder. "Sometimes people don't ever get better. They die sometimes."

I shook my head.

"Not Linda," I said.

But on a September afternoon, during noon recess, Nick Veenhof came up to me on the school playground. "Your girlfriend," he said, "she kicked the bucket."

At first I didn't understand.

"She's dead," he said. "My mom told me at lunch-time. No lie, she actually kicked the goddang *bucket.*"

All I could do was nod. Somehow it didn't quite register. I turned away, glanced down at my hands for a second, then walked home without telling anyone.

It was a little after one o'clock, I remember, and the house was empty.

I drank some chocolate milk and then lay down on the sofa in the living room, not really sad, just floating, trying to imagine what it was to be dead. Nothing much came to me. I remember closing my eyes and whispering her name, almost begging, trying to make her come back. "Linda," I said, "please." And then I concentrated. I willed her alive. It was a dream, I suppose, or a daydream, but I made it happen. I saw her coming down the middle of Main Street, all alone. It was nearly dark and the street was deserted, no cars or people, and Linda wore a pink dress and shiny black shoes. I remember sitting down on the curb to watch. All her hair had grown back. The scars and stitches were gone. In the dream, if that's what it was, she was playing a game of some sort, laughing and running up the empty street, kicking a big aluminum water bucket.

Right then I started to cry. After a moment Linda stopped and carried her water bucket over to the curb and asked why I was so sad.

"Well, God," I said, "you're dead."

Linda nodded at me. She was standing under a yellow streetlight. A nine-year-old girl, just a kid, and yet there was something ageless in her eyes—not a child, not an adult —just a bright ongoing everness, that same pinprick of absolute lasting light that I see today in my own eyes as Timmy smiles at Tim from the graying photographs of that time.

"Dead," I said.

Linda smiled. It was a secret smile, as if she knew things nobody could ever know, and she reached out and touched my wrist and said, "Timmy, stop crying. It doesn't *matter*."

In Vietnam, too, we had ways of making the dead seem not quite so dead. Shaking hands, that was one way. By slighting death, by acting, we pretended it was not the terrible thing it was. By our language, which was both hard and wistful, we transformed the bodies into piles of waste. Thus, when someone got killed, as Curt Lemon did, his body was not really a body, but rather one small bit of waste in the midst of a much wider wastage. I learned that words make a difference. It's easier to cope with a kicked bucket than a corpse; if it isn't human, it doesn't matter much if it's dead. And so a VC nurse, fried by napalm, was a crispy critter. A Vietnamese baby, which lay nearby, was a roasted peanut. "Just a crunchie munchie," Rat Kiley said as he stepped over the body.

We kept the dead alive with stories. When Ted Lavender was shot in the head, the men talked about how they'd never seen him so mellow, how tranquil he was, how it wasn't the bullet but the tranquilizers that blew his mind. He wasn't dead, just laid-back. There were Christians among us, like Kiowa, who believed in the New Testament stories of life after death. Other stories were passed down like legends from old-timer to newcomer. Mostly, though, we had to make up our own. Often they were exaggerated, or blatant lies, but it was a way of bringing body and soul back together, or a way of making new bodies for the souls to inhabit. There was a story, for instance, about how Curt Lemon had gone trick-or-treating on Halloween. A dark, spooky night, and so Lemon put on a ghost mask and painted up his body all different colors and crept across a paddy to a sleeping village—almost stark naked, the story went, just boots and balls and an M-16—and in the dark Lemon went from hootch to hootch—ringing doorbells, he called it—and a few hours later, when he slipped back into the perimeter, he had a whole sackful of goodies to share with his pals: candles and joss sticks and a pair of black pajamas and statuettes of the smiling Buddha. That was the story, anyway. Other versions were much more elaborate, full of descriptions and scraps of dialogue. Rat Kiley liked to spice it up with extra details: "See, what happens is, it's like four in the morning, and Lemon sneaks into a hootch with that weird ghost mask on. Everybody's asleep, right? So he wakes up this cute little mama-san. Tickles her foot. 'Hey, Mama-san,' he goes, real soft like. 'Hey, Mama-san—trick or treat!' Should've seen her face. About freaks. I mean, there's this buck naked ghost standing there, and he's got this M-16 up against her ear and he whispers, 'Hey, Mama-san, trick or fuckin' treat!' Then he takes off her pj's. Strips her right down. Sticks the pajamas in his sack and tucks her into bed and heads for the next hootch."

Pausing a moment, Rat Kiley would grin and shake his head. "Honest to God," he'd murmur. "Trick or treat. Lemon —there's one class act."

To listen to the story, especially as Rat Kiley told it, you'd never know that Curt Lemon was dead. He was still out there in the dark, naked and painted up, trick-or-treating, sliding from hootch to hootch in that crazy white ghost mask. But he was dead.

In September, the day after Linda died, I asked my father to take me down to Benson's Funeral Home to view the body. I was a fifth grader then; I was curious. On the drive downtown my father kept his eyes straight ahead. At one point, I remember, he made a scratchy sound in his throat. It took him a long time to light up a cigarette.

"Timmy," he said, "you're sure about this?"

I nodded at him. Down inside, of course, I wasn't sure, and yet I had to see her one more time. What I needed, I suppose, was some sort of final confirmation, something to carry with me after she was gone.

When we parked in front of the funeral home, my father turned and looked at me. "If this bothers you," he said, "just say the word. We'll make a quick getaway. Fair enough?"

"Okay," I said.

"Or if you start to feel sick or anything—"

"I *won't*," I told him.

Inside, the first thing I noticed was the smell, thick and sweet, like something sprayed out of a can. The viewing room was empty except for Linda and my father and me. I felt a rush of panic as we walked up the aisle. The smell made me dizzy. I tried to fight it off, slowing down a little, taking short, shallow breaths through my mouth. But at the same time I felt a funny excitement. Anticipation, in a way—that same awkward feeling as when I'd walked up the sidewalk to ring her doorbell on our first date. I wanted to impress her. I wanted something to happen between us, a secret signal of some sort. The room was dimly lighted, almost dark, but at the far end of the aisle Linda's white casket was illuminated by a row of spotlights up in the ceiling. Everything was quiet. My father put his hand on my shoulder, whispered something, and backed off. After a moment I edged forward a few steps, pushing up on my toes for a better look.

It didn't seem real. A mistake, I thought. The girl lying in the white casket wasn't Linda. There was a resemblance, maybe, but where Linda had always been very slender and fragile-looking, almost skinny, the body in that casket was fat and swollen. For a second I wondered if somebody had made a terrible blunder. A technical mistake: pumped her too full of formaldehyde or embalming fluid or whatever they used. Her arms and face were bloated. The skin at her cheeks was stretched out tight like the rubber skin on a balloon just before it pops open. Even her fingers seemed puffy. I turned and glanced behind me, where my father stood, thinking that maybe it was a joke—hoping it was a joke—almost believing that Linda would jump out from behind one of the curtains and laugh and yell out my name.

But she didn't. The room was silent. When I looked back at the casket, I felt dizzy again. In my heart, I'm sure, I knew this was Linda, but even so I couldn't find much to recognize. I tried to pretend she was taking a nap, her hands folded at her stomach, just sleeping away the afternoon. Except she didn't *look* asleep. She looked dead. She looked heavy and totally dead.

I remember closing my eyes. After a while my father stepped up beside me.

"Come on now," he said. "Let's go get some ice cream."

In the months after Ted Lavender died, there were many other bodies. I never shook hands—not that—but one afternoon I climbed a tree and threw down what was left of Curt Lemon. I watched my friend Kiowa sink into the muck along the Song Tra Bong. And in early July, after a battle in the mountains, I was assigned to a six-man detail to police up the enemy KIAs. There were twenty-seven bodies altogether, and parts of several others. The dead were everywhere. Some lay in piles. Some lay alone. One, I remember, seemed to kneel. Another was bent from the waist over a small boulder, the top of his head on the ground, his arms rigid, the eyes squinting in concentration as if he were about to perform a handstand or somersault. It was my worst day at the war. For three hours we carried the bodies down the mountain to a clearing alongside a narrow dirt road. We had lunch there, then a truck pulled up, and we worked in two-man teams to load the truck. I remember swinging the bodies up. Mitchell Sanders took a man's feet, I took the arms, and we counted to three, working up momentum, and then we tossed the body high and watched it bounce and come to rest among the other bodies. The dead had been dead for more than a day. They were all badly bloated. Their clothing was stretched tight like sausage skins, and when we picked them up, some made sharp burping sounds as the gases were released. They were heavy. Their feet were bluish green and cold. The smell was terrible. At one point Mitchell Sanders looked at me and said, "Hey, man, I just realized something."

"What?"

He wiped his eyes and spoke very quietly, as if awed by his own wisdom.

"Death sucks," he said.

Lying in bed at night, I made up elaborate stories to bring Linda alive in my sleep. I invented my own dreams. It sounds impossible, I know, but I did it. I'd picture somebody's birthday party—a crowded room, I'd think, and a big chocolate cake with pink candles—and then soon I'd be dreaming it, and after a while Linda would show up, as I knew she would, and in the dream we'd look at each other and not talk much, because we were shy, but then later I'd walk her home and we'd sit on her front steps and stare at the dark and just be together.

She'd say amazing things sometimes. "Once you're alive," she'd say, "you can't ever be dead."

Or she'd say: "Do I *look* dead?"

It was a kind of self-hypnosis. Partly willpower, partly faith, which is how stories arrive.

But back then it felt like a miracle. My dreams had become a secret meeting place, and in the weeks after she died I couldn't wait to fall asleep at night. I began going to bed earlier and earlier, sometimes even in bright daylight. My mother, I remember, finally asked about it at breakfast one morning. "Timmy, what's *wrong*?" she said, but all I could do was shrug and say, "Nothing. I just need sleep, that's all." I didn't dare tell the truth. It was embarrassing, I suppose, but it was also a precious secret, like a magic trick, where if I tried to explain it, or even talk about it, the thrill and mystery would be gone. I didn't want to lose Linda.

She was dead. I understood that. After all, I'd seen her body. And yet even as a nine-year-old I had begun to practice the magic of stories. Some I just dreamed up. Others I wrote down—the scenes and dialogue. And at nighttime I'd slide into sleep knowing that Linda would be there waiting for me. Once, I remember, we went ice skating late at night, tracing loops and circles under yellow floodlights. Later we sat by a wood stove in the warming house, all alone, and after a while I asked her what it was like to be dead. Apparently Linda thought it was a silly question. She smiled and said, "Do I *look* dead?"

I told her no, she looked terrific. I waited a moment, then

asked again, and Linda made a soft little sigh. I could smell our wool mittens drying on the stove.

For a few seconds she was quiet.

"Well, right now," she said, "I'm *not* dead. But when I am, it's like . . . I don't know, I guess it's like being inside a book that nobody's reading."

"A book?" I said.

"An old one. It's up on a library shelf, so you're safe and everything, but the book hasn't been checked out for a long, long time. All you can do is wait. Just hope somebody'll pick it up and start reading."

Linda smiled at me.

"Anyhow, it's not so bad," she said. "I mean, when you're dead, you just have to be yourself." She stood up and put on her red stocking cap. "This is stupid. Let's go skate some more."

So I followed her down to the frozen pond. It was late, and nobody else was there, and we held hands and skated almost all night under the yellow lights.

And then it becomes 1990. I'm forty-three years old, and a writer now, still dreaming Linda alive in exactly the same way. She's not the embodied Linda; she's mostly made up, with a new identity and a new name, like the man who never was. Her real name doesn't matter. She was nine years old. I loved her and then she died. And yet right here, in the spell of memory and imagination, I can still see her as if through ice, as if I'm gazing into some other world, a place where there are no brain tumors and no funeral homes, where there are no bodies at all. I can see Kiowa, too, and Ted Lavender and Curt Lemon, and sometimes I can even see Timmy skating with Linda under the yellow floodlights.

I'm young and happy. I'll never die. I'm skimming across the surface of my own history, moving fast, riding the melt beneath the blades, doing loops and spins, and when I take a high leap into the dark and come down thirty years later, I realize it is as Tim trying to save Timmy's life with a story.